SOMETHING FOR THE PAIN

NEW YORK TIMES AND USA TODAY BESTSELLING AUTHOR

VICTORIA ASHLEY

SOMETHING FOR THE PAIN

Copyright © 2015 Victoria Ashley

Cover Artist: Designs by Dana

Photographer: Wander Aguiar

Model: Thane W.

Editor: Charisse Spiers

Formatter: N. E. Henderson

SOMETHING FOR THE PAIN

NEW YORK TIMES AND USA TODAY BESTSELLING AUTHOR

VICTORIA ASHLEY

ONE

ALEX

ZIPPING UP THE FLY OF my favorite denims, I hop into my truck while apologizing to Jade. Things were just starting to get heated when I heard my phone go off and saw that it was Tripp. I tried my hardest to ignore it, but every time she calls, I let my heart do the talking . . . even *when* I am naked and rock hard.

Shit! That is going to hurt later.

When I answered, she had asked me to meet her at our favorite bar. She said it was important, which leads to why I am now sitting in my truck with an angry Jade throwing my shirt at my head.

"Who does that, huh?" Slipping on her heels, she leans in and grips the top of my window as I toss my shirt into the passenger seat. She lets out a deep breath and looks away, embarrassed. "No man in his right mind leaves during sex to go see another woman. What makes you think this opportunity is going to come up again? Do you just assume that you'll get another chance?" She turns back to face me again while brushing her black hair behind her ear. "Well do you, Alex? Huh?"

I shove my key into the ignition and watch her chest as it quickly rises and falls. She sounds irate, but her eyes are full of want and need as they scan over my tatted chest and arms. Her body is still craving my touch and wanting more; it's clear as fucking day. From the way her body was reacting to mine in the bedroom, there is no doubt in my mind that if I *wanted* this to happen again, it would. The question is, do I *want* it to happen again?

"Look, Jade. I already explained this to you. When a friend calls and says they need me . . . I go. Not that it's any of your business, but I've known Tripp since I was eight. If she needs me, there is nothing that is going to stop me from going." I bring my eyes down to her breasts and lick my lips. As turned on as I may be, my head overrules my dick when it comes to Tripp. "Not even some very *dirty* sex." I turn the key, starting up the engine and a small growl escapes from her throat. "Save the growling for the bedroom."

Running her tongue over her perfectly bleached teeth, she takes a step back and places her hands to her hips as I pull out of her driveway. There is no doubt that she is pissed to the max, but she'll get over it. They always do. This isn't the first time I have left during the middle of sex to take care of Tripp. It won't be the last time either. In the past I've left elevator sex, office sex, bathroom stall sex . . . basically sex in any place you can think of. This is the norm for *us*. This is how we've always been, how we function.

When I arrive at *Blue's*, I jump out of my truck, slip my shirt over my head, and yank the back door open. It's pretty close to empty, so I spot Tripp immediately after I step inside. She's already seated in the far-left side, our usual spot.

Her eyes lock with mine and seeing them light up is all the confirmation I need to know that I made the right decision by coming. It's always the right decision when it comes to her.

"Holy shit, Alex. I think that was a record." She glances down at her phone. "It took a total of five minutes and thirty-nine seconds. Don't I just feel special." Her full, slightly pink lips turn up into a smile as she stands and walks over to me.

I can't help but notice how hot she looks today, in her little white dress. It's short and tight, molding to her curvy, tanned body. That sight does things to men, uncontrollable things. I must admit to myself that I have never met anyone more beautiful in my life than her. Everything from her little freckled nose to the intensity of her big, blue eyes screams perfection to me.

She throws her arms around me and I pull her close, out of instinct. The soft smell of vanilla is present, her usual choice of shampoo and body wash. I never get tired of her scent. I'm around her so much that the smell even haunts me in my dreams.

After a few seconds she pulls away and slowly runs her hand through my hair with a light tug. I love my hair being tugged. It's on my top list of shit that turns me on, and for some reason she knows exactly how I like it.

Her small nose scrunches, making a cute face as her eyes take me in. "From the looks of your messy hair I would say I interrupted someone being a *dirty* boy again . . . no?"

She leans in and places her nose against my neck, running it just under my ear and stopping. Goose bumps rise on my flesh as she takes in a deep breath and moans, before pulling away and licking her lips. It's so seductive and she probably doesn't even realize it. "And you smell delicious, so I'm guessing I am right? I take it a lot of girls are getting tattoos these days."

They are, but I won't get into that with her.

Walking over to the small booth, I avoid her question, take a seat, and wait for her to take one across from me. I need to get my thoughts in order and keep my control in check. It's not easy just leaving while you're balls deep between a pair of long, slender thighs and not getting a chance to even finish. I reach for the Miller Lite that she has waiting for me, hold it up to my lips, and tilt it back while adjusting myself under the table.

With curious eyes, she takes a sip of her Daiquiri and eyes me up and down with slight amusement. "I'm going to take that as a yes to my question. I know you too damn well, stud. No words are needed."

"Yeah . . . And she was pretty upset too. She practically chased me outside in the nude. I'm lucky she didn't stab my dick with her heel." I set my beer down in front of me and give her a questioning look as she grins and covers her mouth. I wait for her to tell me what the hell was so important, but she just takes another sip of her drink before licking the red slush from her lips and playing with her straw, as if we could just sit here all day. She's trying to put off telling me something, but she can't hide shit from me. "So . . ." I push. "Tell me."

She lets out a little laugh. "Is someone a little impatient today?" She asks while getting comfortable in her seat, trying to pretend that nothing is up. "We don't have anywhere to be. Well . . . at least I don't."

"You said it was important. What's up, Tripp? You and Lucas breaking up?" I raise an eyebrow and try to look concerned, but inside I'm fucking thrilled and hoping that I'm right. She's too good for him, but she's too blind to notice.

Her smile only broadens as she shakes her head. "Oh come on. You know that's not it, and technically we're not a couple. I mean . . . it's nothing serious, yet. Don't make me say it again." She pauses and starts playing with the end of her ponytail. She always does that when she's nervous. It's fucking adorable, making me want to reach across the table and pull her into my lap. "Actually . . . Lucas asked me to move in with him the other day. He found a good deal on a really awesome house and wants to get out of his apartment. I have to admit, it's hard to pass up."

You have got to be shitting me.

Her words stop my fucking heart, taking me a few seconds to respond. "Please tell me you said no." I take a long swig of my beer and swallow, before taking another one, while looking her straight in the eyes. The way my heart is racing right now is making me uncomfortable, leaving me uneasy. I don't like where this conversation is headed. "You *did* say no, right?"

"Alex! Why would I say no? This is a great opportunity to get out of my aunt's house. I just turned twenty-one. Who in their right mind would choose staying at home over freedom? Come on."

"I'll give you one good reason. The only one that you need, and you know I would never steer you wrong."

She leans over the table and puts her face close to mine. Her eyes bounce back and forth between mine, challenging me. "Oh yeah, Alex Carter. What is that reason? You always seem to know what's *best* for me. Go ahead, enlighten me."

I lean in closer so my lips are almost brushing hers, then I stop and wet them. I see her eyes dart down to my lips before she looks up nervously and focuses her attention back on my eyes. In a small moment of weakness, I almost flick my tongue out and run it across her lips but stop myself from making that mistake. "You've been *dating* for less than a year. You're too young to move in with a guy, with this guy. It's a horrible idea. I don't agree with this shit, Tripp. I can't."

She rubs her nose against mine, before kissing it and

smiling as if she already knew exactly what I was going to say and already has her answer perfectly planned out. I'm not surprised. "That is exactly why we will have separate rooms. It's a three-bedroom home with an indoor and outdoor pool. It even has an extra room, big enough for a pool table and gym equipment... or anything that you want. It's the perfect party house. We are young and wild, right. I want to live that way for once. It's time to have fun and loosen up before settling down and doing this grown up shit."

Running my hand through my hair, I take a drink of my beer and shake my head in aggravation. "I don't like the idea of you guys living alone together, Tripp. I know you're not exactly a couple, *but* he might start to get possessive of you once he gets that taste of what it's like to have you every day. I don't trust you in his hands. He doesn't deserve you and my opinion on that won't change."

"Are you serious, Alex?" She sounds a bit shocked and confused. She's not too happy with me at the moment, but she'll get over it and see my point of view. She usually does. I'm always honest with her, even if it does hurt her feelings. I can't be anything but. Honesty is what she needs. "I have known Lucas since I was fifteen. You have known him since you were sixteen. I don't get what your problem is."

"Yeah, and *I* have known *you* since I was eight. It's my job to protect you. I don't see you guys moving in together as being a good idea. I don't like it and I don't think you should do it."

She stands up and walks over to slide next to me in the

booth. She wraps her arms around my waist and leans her head on my shoulder, looking up at me. "What if I told you that it wouldn't just be the two of us? Would it make you feel any better about it?"

I tilt my head down and strain my eyes to look into hers. I like that idea just a little bit more than the first, *but* it's still not enough for me to like it, however I'll let her finish anyway. "I'm listening."

"We want you to move in with us. My first place just wouldn't seem right without you being there. It will be fun. I promise."

I let out a breath of frustration and shake my head. I didn't see this shit coming and I really have no idea what to think. "It sounds complicated as shit, babe. The three of us as roommates . . . and he's okay with that? You don't see him getting jealous when I walk around the house nude and shit, getting your attention? I wouldn't want to put him to shame. It might crush his spirit."

She elbows me in the side, causing me to jump away and spit out the drink of beer that I had just taken. Looking down at my now wet shirt, she covers her mouth and laughs. "You don't walk around nude, so shut up." She sits up and looks at me with questioning eyes, as I lift my eyebrows in disagreement. *Someone's curiosity is piqued.* "Or do you? Have I been missing something?"

"You really want to find out?" I question with a smirk.

She lets out a nervous laugh before turning around in the booth to face me, pressing her knee against my leg. She grabs my thigh and squeezes it to let me know she wants me to get serious. "Look. You know what kind of relationship Lucas and I have. What part of that makes you think he will get jealous? Plus, he knows we are *only* friends. We spend every day together and he has never once complained. We have an understanding for the time being and it works. Trust me."

I lean back against the wall and steel my jaw, while studying her eyes. Everything about them makes me want to break down. "Yeah. I still don't agree on your little arrangement, but because I know you so well, I understand. I just wish it could be different."

Tripp has had a shitty childhood, and I don't blame her for not getting close to many people. I understand that way too much. Her druggie parents abandoned her at the age of seven and she has been living with her aunt Tara since. When I met her, she felt alone and crushed. Her aunt had a job that kept her busy most of the time and she had no other family. I became her family. I took care of her.

When her and Lucas hooked up less than a year ago and it started getting emotionally weighted, she told him she wasn't ready to commit, but that she really liked him. She just couldn't let him in or open up. In turn she felt selfish for not being able to give him all her time, so she decided it was best to not get serious for a while. They both agreed on an open relationship as long as they were both honest with each other. I didn't like it then and I still don't.

Most of all I hated that she had to be so selfless to make him happy. If he cared about her enough, then he shouldn't have agreed to the ridiculous shit they are—using one another. He should have just told her he would wait for her. I would have.

She squeezes my leg tighter and scoots closer. "I know. I know. I asked him to just be patient and give us a year. We are both young and I'm in no rush to be anything serious. I know you don't understand the reasoning behind why Lucas and I have this relationship. It just works for us. I don't feel pressure for more and it's fun. I don't feel like I have to pretend with him like so many others, you know. He doesn't push me or take more than I'm willing to give. We're both okay with that." She stops to flash me a devilish grin. "Hell . . . we even mess around with other people sometimes just to get worked up for each other. It's such a damn rush. So as you can see there is nothing for Lucas to be jealous about when he can take it out on someone else. It will be fine."

I almost finish my beer off and let all her information sink in. Why does this shit piss me off? All this time I thought it was only Lucas having fun on the side. I never thought to ask her about it. "Alright, let me get this straight. So you let these other guys put their hands on you and Lucas just lets them without wanting to strangle them?"

My chest hurts at the thought. I have a strong instinct to protect her. The thought of other men getting off on her just for the hell of it pisses me off. "You never told me that shit. I didn't think you needed it. I can't say I like this little game either. I hope you're using protection. Shit, Tripp."

"It's not as bad as you make it sound. Just because I'm a

girl, it doesn't mean that I shouldn't be allowed to have a little fun once in a while too. You have your fun, and I don't judge you." She shakes her head and pushes my arm, offended. She does have a point there. I have no right to judge her, but it's hard as hell. "We're young, Alex. There is nothing wrong with exploring. It's only happened like two times, but you get the point. It's not like I suck them off or have sex or anything, jeez. It's just kissing and a little touching. Lucas is the only one I have slept with and we always use protection. Always."

Still, I can't help but picture her doing dirty things to other men. The thought infuriates me. The bigger shocker is that I'm surprised he allows it, and that he wants it too. I would fucking kill someone if I were in his shoes. I always knew there was something wrong with that dick's head.

"Yeah, well if I were your man . . ." I pause to tilt back my beer. "You better believe I would be the only one pleasuring you. I protect and take care of what is mine, and you wouldn't need other men to please you. I would be yours . . . anytime, anyway, and any fucking where."

Her face turns red, and for a brief second, I can see her trying to catch her breath. My words had an effect on her, and I'm not sure what that means, or what I want it to mean.

"But that's just me." I add. "You know what kind of man I am. I don't share. I guess if that's what gets you off, then why not?"

"Why do you sound so mad? You knew what kind of *relationship* Lucas and I had. Nothing in regard to Lucas and I has ever been set in stone. We're just having fun while we can. There's no reason to be mad. It all stops soon and then we both have to decide what to do from there. We either both fully commit, or we just stay friends. This was an easy way to keep things light instead of ruining our friendship if it didn't work out. Less pressure on both of us."

She takes a long sip of her drink, while watching me with curious eyes.

I'm more than mad. The thought of Lucas treating her that way makes me want to choke the life out of him. "I just don't get how Lucas has known you for six years and he doesn't have the same urge to protect you as I do. Tripp, I would hurt anyone that hurt you. You mean more to me than just fun. I've watched you grow up over the last thirteen years. You're one of the most important people in my life. I've always been there for you and always will be. Even when I left . . . to take care of that shit, I still called you and worried about you almost every day. Things have changed a little since then but not really. The only thing different is that you're in a *relationship* now, or fucking him at least. I'm still your best fucking friend. I will always protect you."

She's right. It's not as bad as I make it sound, but I can't help it. The thought of more than one guy being able to touch her makes my blood boil. I understand her completely, but at the moment, I'm choosing not to.

She grabs my arm and rests her head on it. "That's why I love you so much. I know that you will protect me and the same goes for you. I will always have your back. That's why

I don't only *want* you to move in with us, but I *need* you to. I know you're making enough money at the tattoo shop and that being in that house still hurts you. Come stay with me, please. Let Memphis and Lyric take the house. It will be fun. I promise."

I look at her and swallow, but don't say a word. My head is spinning so fast right now that I want to throw my fist into a wall. This is stupid. I'm going to make a stupid decision because I care about her too much. I have a feeling that being in the same house with them and seeing Lucas bring home other girls is going to make me despise him, even if she does say it's *their* thing. Not to mention Tripp bringing other guys as well. I can't handle that shit.

"Please! I know you love to swim. You can bring as many girls to the house as you want. You can even have sex in the pool, and I won't even care. I just want you there. Anything goes . . . "

I suck in my bottom lip and smirk at the picture in my head. I guess it doesn't seem all that bad when she puts it that way. Plus, I can look out for her. "What girls?"

"Oh please." She grins. "You don't just have girls begging to get into your pants. You have girls biting each other's heads off like zombie bitches to get a taste. I'm pretty sure there have been a few fights to the death for you. You're sexy as sin and you fucking know it." She pokes at my cheeks and smiles when I smile. "Look at those sexy dimples and strikingly handsome features. I have seen you grow up from a dangly little boy with scraggily hair to one of the sexiest men I have ever laid eyes on. I tell you this all the time. You know I hold nothing back. Please, my gorgeously handsome best friend." She gives me puppy dog eyes and bats her long, thick lashes at me.

And just like that, I'm hers, and I'll do just about anything that she asks. Plus, she's right. I think it's time I let Memphis and Lyric have some privacy. *Fuck!* She knows how to work me. "So where is this damn house?"

She practically jumps out of her seat with excitement. "I knew that would get you. It always does." She grabs my hand and pulls me out of the booth. "I have a key. I'll take you there now so you can check it out."

"Alright," I huff, while tossing down some cash. "This better be fucking good, Tripp . . . And this is the last time that eye batting shit will work on me."

"Uh huh, sure." She smiles, knowing that I'm full of shit. "Follow me, Stud."

What the hell am I getting myself into?

TWO

TRIPP

MY HEART IS RACING SO hard that it's making it hard to concentrate on the road. Alex is following behind me in his massive truck and I can't stop looking back at him through the rearview mirror to check his expressions. I never meant for him to get upset about Lucas asking me to move in with him, or about our open *relationship*. There was no way I would have agreed to live with Lucas unless I knew for a fact that Alex would move in as well. Alex and I just have that connection. He would do just about anything for me and the same goes for me over him.

We have experienced everything together growing up, even our first kiss. Even though I was only eleven and he twelve, still, it was with him. Nothing can replace that. I was so scared that no one would want to kiss me. As soon as I told Alex about my fear, he smiled, licked his lips, and pulled me in for a kiss. It was soft, heartwarming, and over before I could breathe. We never spoke of it again, but it still haunts me to this day. I may have been young, but the spark I felt was unforgettable. He stepped up and made sure I knew that he cared and would always be there for me. I love him for that. Always will.

This . . . this is no different for me. I really do want him here for this big moment again. I want my first real place to be with him. He's my world and he knows it. The only first I couldn't give him was my virginity, because it would have ruined everything. I can't even picture losing him as my best friend, and that's what would happen by letting my feelings or sexual attraction for him get in the way. That is exactly why I gave it to Lucas instead. Alex means too much.

Pulling up in front of the huge brick house, I smile and kill the engine as I look behind me to see Alex pull up halfway in the grass. He's always been good at shitty parking. I know he does it on purpose, but after all these years it still makes me laugh.

He jumps out of his truck and runs his hand through his thick, dark hair, before pulling my car door open and reaching for my hand. "You had better sell me on this house, Tripp. It better be good enough to make my cock hard."

I can't help my eyes as they look down at the crotch of his fitted jeans. *Damn, those are some nice jeans.* He catches me looking, so I quickly pull my eyes away and clear my throat, as if that makes it any less obvious. I'm not a shy person, but I'm trying my best with him. I need him too much to ruin what we have. "Oh trust me. This house even gives me a lady boner. You will love it."

His hand quickly reaches behind me to shut my car door. Then he flashes me a sexy grin, pops his neck, and pulls me by my hand. "It's that good, huh?"

I don't even get a chance to answer, before he reaches down and snatches the key that is hanging down in front of me. I feel the back of his hand accidently brush against my private, giving me instant goose bumps. "Hey. Watch it. That was pretty damn close to my..."

He licks his lips and his eyes trail down my body. "Pussy," he growls. "I know."

My face heats and I can barely even speak "Yeah . . . no, I mean . . ." I take a deep breath. "Just watch yourself, Carter."

He chuckles as he sticks the key into the lock. "I was looking for your *lady boner.*"

He opens the door and then looks back at me with a sly grin. *Fuck me, those dimples do things to a woman's body.* "I didn't find it. I guess next time I'll have to search deeper."

The intensity of his gray eyes lock with mine, causing me to swallow hard and try to hide my blushing face. I don't know if he has figured it out over the years, but his words and teasing leave me extremely hot and bothered. I try my best to hide it, because I know he's only joking, but the fact that it sometimes makes it hard to breathe is definitely something I have stopped trying to internally deny. Hiding it from my best friend is almost as hard as not breathing. I find it extremely hard to hide anything from him at all.

"Well, lead the way, beautiful." He steps back and leans against the door with his legs crossed in front of him. "I'm waiting to get hard."

I laugh softly, but turn my face away to get better control over my wandering eyes. "And how will I know if it makes you hard?" I tilt my head a little in question, but keep my eyes looking straight ahead.

"Oh you will see it. Trust me." I hear the door close before I feel his body pressed against mine. He's so close, yet not close enough. I want him to touch me. I crave it. Just once. "So far, I'm not impressed."

I spin around with quickness and look up at him, about to hand him his ass. "What do you mean?" His face turns up into a smile to show me that he's only trying to work me up, so shutting my mouth I give his chest a shove. It doesn't even make him shift. Not a single inch. Not like when we were kids and we used to play fight. Back then he was tall and twig like, giving me an actual chance. Now . . . mmm . . . now he is all man: tall, thick, strong, and sexy. "You seriously need to stop working out so much. I can barely even move you now. Is that all you do when you're not tattooing."

He bites his bottom lip and crosses his arms across his firm chest. "That and have sex. What the hell else am I supposed to be doing? I'm kind of limited." I watch his teeth as they dig into his full bottom lip before letting go. He's always had a thing for biting his bottom lip. Doesn't he realize how damn sexy and distracting that is? I'm sure he must be aware of it.

So. Stop. It.

"Okay . . . you could have kept that to yourself." I wave my arms around, motioning around the huge empty space, preparing to give him a tour. "Well, this is the living room, as you can see. It's a good size. Fireplace over here, huge picture windows over there, and it leads straight into the kitchen." I turn behind me. "This way over to the right leads to the stairs and the hallway."

He looks around with his arms crossed and his forehead crinkled. His almost silver eyes are unreadable at the moment. He's trying to make me nervous. He knows he's got a good poker face too. I hate it!

I exhale and start walking towards the kitchen with him following at my heels. "Alright, pain in the ass. You're playing hardball. Maybe the kitchen will better impress you."

Alex steps in behind me and looks around. His eyes scan over the stainless-steel stove and fridge before his eyes stop on the bar in the back-right corner. His eyebrows scrunch together in thought. "Are you going to be our sexy little bartender?"

He takes a few steps toward the bar and stops in front of it. I step up beside him, and before I can speak, he picks me up by the hips and sets me down on top of the bar. He grins at the sight of me and then releases my hips. "Or you can just sit there and look pretty. Either way, I think the kitchen is my favorite so far. He looks down at his jeans and bites his bottom lip. "It's getting harder by the second, but I need it to be rock hard. That's not going to be easy. Come on, Tripp." He picks me up and sets me back down to my feet. I can't help but take notice of his hands lingering for a few seconds too long. "Show me this *sex* pool you told me about. If that doesn't do the trick, then I don't know what will."

Closing my eyes for a quick second, I take a breath and exhale before following him back into the living room and down the hall. The thought of his dick hard is now clouding my thoughts. How the hell am I going to sell him on this house when all I can think about is having him inside of me?

He stops walking and turns around to look at me so I can lead him to the right room. I give him a half smile and pass him up. I walk to the very back of the hallway and push the double doors open. The smell of chlorine hits me hard and the moisture in the air makes me smile. He has to fall in love with this room.

"This is the pool; one of them at least. It's pretty private back here, so it shouldn't be a problem for you to bring your girlies over. You won't be bothered."

He looks at me, smiles, and then walks past me and into the room. "Hell yes," he groans. "It's fucking hard now, Tripp."

I feel my stomach flutter and my heart rate pick up from his choice of words. I can't tell if it's because I am happy that he's going to agree to moving in or because the thought of him hard makes me want to jump on him and take him for a ride. He's my best friend, but dammit I still want to. I shouldn't even be questioning myself, but I can't help it.

"Umm . . . good, I guess," I say in response as I step up beside him in front of the water.

When I look down at his hand, I notice him adjusting the crotch of his jeans. I give him a shove and he looks over at me with a grin. "Damn, Tripp. Are you trying to make me wrestle you? You know it's been a while, but you've been pretty damn pushy today. I still have the skills to take you down."

I can't help but to laugh. "I pushed you because you were playing with your dick. Are you seriously hard right now?"

He pulls his hand away from his jeans and sure enough I see a huge bulge. I can tell it's not fully hard, but *damn!* "Well, what the hell do you expect when you call this the sex pool? Am I not supposed to get aroused at the thought of fucking someone in here?"

I pull my eyes away from his crotch and punch his arm. "Oh come on, Tripp. Don't be ashamed to look. We've known each other our whole lives. You don't really think I haven't sneaked peeks at your body from time to time, do you? Don't lie to me. You know you've imagined how big it is before. I'll even give you a look if you want. What's mine is yours," he says huskily.

Why is that sexy?

He bites his bottom lip and reaches for his belt as he steps closer to me in a teasing way. The thought of his erection being so close to me has me so nervous that I reach out with both hands and push him into the pool. My hands instantly go up to cover my mouth as he falls in with a huge splash.

I burst out in laughter as he quickly resurfaces and jumps out of the pool, while wiping his face off. His shirt is clinging to his muscular body and water is dripping down his face and lips. It's the most glorious sight I have ever seen. Just when I think he's about to yell at me, he yanks his shirt over his head and reaches into his pocket to toss his phone aside. He grins and closes the distance between us.

"You're getting it now." I take in a deep breath as his cold, firm chest presses against my breasts. "You ready for me to get you wet, Tripp? I've been waiting for this for a long, *long* time."

He's too quick for me to even attempt to make an escape. He picks me up, wraps my legs around his waist, and walks over the edge of the pool. I instantly take notice of his partial erection pressing firmly between my legs, which only makes me wish we were naked.

We sink to the bottom with his hands gripping onto my bare thighs as he holds me close. As soon as his feet hit the bottom of the pool, he pushes up with his muscular legs and we both swim back up to the surface.

I fight to catch my breath while wiping water off my face. "Dammit, Alex!"

I hear him laughing behind me, so I turn around to yell at him, but he's too quick and is already back behind me again. "What's the matter? You didn't expect me to get you so wet?"

I lean my head back and bite my lip in frustration. Him

and this damn teasing. He's really getting a kick out of this. "You're lucky I love you so much," I bite out.

I feel his body press behind me, before he wraps his arm around me and starts pulling me back to the edge of the pool. Once there, he picks me up and gives my ass a boost until I am on my knees, catching my breath on the smooth, wet cement. My body gets heated from the skin to skin contact and feeling his finger so close to slipping inside me. All it would take is one little nudge. It's the closest it's been before and it steals my breath away. I chose to wear a thong today, so not only did my dress ride up, but also I'm sure he just got a full on view of my ass in his face.

I quickly get back to my feet and turn around to face him, now embarrassed. He's just standing there, staring up at me, his eyes unreadable. "Aren't you getting out?"

His eyes quickly scan over my breasts before moving down to my exposed thighs and staying there. "Yeah. I'm coming." He smiles and I give him the middle finger. "No, I didn't mean it like that." He laughs while pulling himself halfway out of the pool. "You have such a dirty mind," he says in a serious tone. "I'm not sure I can handle living with someone with such filthy thoughts. You just might corrupt me."

I place my foot on his shoulder and give him a shove back into the water. He comes up laughing and flashes me his charming smile; the one that gets any and every girl in bed. For me, this smile makes me forgive him for anything that he ever does; it lets him get away with *everything*. This smile melts my heart. It's the one thing that kept me sane as a child. Whenever I was sad he would flash that smile and point at his dimples and all of my worries disappeared. Now, he just flashes the smile. It still has the same effect.

"Come on, Alex. Stop teasing me. You know I will be devastated if you don't move in. I already have your room picked out."

He smiles up at me and jumps out of the pool. I stand here in silence for a moment and watch as he wipes the water down his firm, tatted chest. I've always loved the way his muscles flex whenever he moves. I find it sexy and hypnotizing, especially now that he's wet. It almost makes me wish that he were just a stranger, with no strong connection, so that I could have just one night to do anything that I please with his body. That would be to have him and no consequences afterward. I never once expected Alex to grow up to be so painfully sexy.

Oh the things I would do to you if I could.

"Well, when you put it that way . . ." He walks over and kisses my forehead while wrapping his arms around my head and squeezing. "How can I say no? Show me to my room."

"Thank you!" I grab him by his arm and start pulling him through the room excitedly.

He pulls me back a few times to slow me down and catches me when I almost slip. "Careful, Firecracker. I don't want to have to rush you to the emergency room before I get to see my room."

I slow down and turn back for my sandals when I realize

that they are now in the pool. *Screw all that.* Then I look down at his black Chucks that are soaking wet and laugh to myself. "Why do you still call me firecracker? I colored my hair red once when I was fifteen."

He picks up a strand of my hair and examines it. "Your hair has always reminded me of a shiny new penny with all the copper tones in it. Even under all that brown and copper though, there has always been red in your hair. You can only really see it in the sun though. I like it. And plus, your face always turns all red when I tease you. You'll always be my firecracker."

I shake my head and roll my eyes. "Oh yeah. Why don't you just write a song about it." I tease. "That sounded pretty deep coming from *your* mouth."

He follows me down the hall toward the stairs. "Maybe I will. You know I still play my guitar each night. I can't write songs for shit but for you I would try."

I stop and he does the same. I look him up and down, standing there shirtless and wet as I try to hold back my desire to kiss him. Our eyes meet for a split second before I pull myself out of my trance, clear my throat, and reach for the railing. "Alright," I say, changing the subject and my thought process. "Well, there are two rooms upstairs," I continue, as he follows me up with his hands on my hips for support. "The other one is downstairs and down the hall from the pool and rec room."

We stop in front of the first door and I reach for the handle, but then stop and smile at him. "This one . . . is *not* your room." I head for the back of the hall and his smile broadens, because he loves being teased. "This here is your room."

He walks past me and pushes the door open. His eyes widen as he takes in the sight before him. "Wow! Did you do all of this?"

He walks over to the wall by the window and touches one of his own favorite drawings that I attempted to paint. Yesterday, I spent the whole day painting music notes and some of his drawings onto the back wall of his room. I even brought his favorite plush pillow that he leaves at my aunt's house so he can sit on it whenever he plays his guitar for me.

"Yeah. I just thought it would be a nice spot for you to have to play your guitar." I walk over and open the window. "You can sit here with the window open and play for the cars passing by."

I plop down onto his pillow—chair—thing. I'm really not sure what to call it. It's not really any of the above, but a mixture. "Like how you used to when we were teenagers. Do you remember? Right before your mom..." I stop myself and clear my throat. "I remember you sitting on your screened in porch by the window, playing all night. I would sometimes drive over late at night just to listen to you play. It helped me sleep better. Actually, you were sitting in that same spot, attempting to play Memphis' guitar the day we met. Remember?"

He smiles to himself and then grabs my hand to help me to my feet. "Of course I remember that shit."

He plops down on his huge pillow and pulls me down onto his lap, and then adjusts me to make sure I'm comfortable before speaking. "I was sitting there playing the guitar and I was so pissed off because I kept messing up, so I decided to quit. Then I heard a little voice coming from outside the window say something like, "Please play some more." I looked out and there you were; the cutest little girl with a penny colored ponytail. It was the shiniest damn hair I had ever seen. My father was gone . . . at work, so I played some more."

We both laugh as he wraps his arms around my waist and squeezes. "Is that your room down the hall?" He asks with a hint of humor.

I lean my head against his shoulder and smile. "Yes. You know I have to be upstairs. We even get to share a connecting bathroom." I point to the bathroom door. "That leads into the bathroom and my room is on the other side. We'll just have to be sure to lock both doors so we know when the other is using it."

He brushes my hair out of the way before resting his scruffy chin on my shoulder. "Why did you choose for my room to be upstairs instead of Lucas'?"

I twist my neck back to look at him. "Because it reminds me of when we were kids and you used to climb through my window. Hell, I still catch you climbing through my bedroom window instead of using the door. You know Tara doesn't mind you coming over whenever you want. We are *adults* now."

We both stop laughing and look up when we hear footsteps enter the room.

Lucas looks down at us and flashes a half smile. "You two having fun without me?"

I feel Alex stiffen beneath me, and then he helps me to my feet before getting up as well.

"Lucas," Alex mutters while pushing the pillow back against the wall. "We were just breaking in my room."

I shake my head and laugh while giving Alex a light shove. I know that it doesn't bother Lucas, but sometimes I wonder why he makes those kinds of jokes so often. "Shut up, dick-lick."

Lucas brushes his blonde hair out of his face and nods his head at me with a chuckle. "Dick-lick?" He raises an eyebrow and heads for the door. "That's a new one." He stops in the doorway and waits for us to join him. "I see you guys have already taken a dip in the pool. I'm also guessing that she's talked you into saying yes?"

Alex runs his tongue over his bottom lip and nods his head as if trying to hold something back. "Do you even have to ask?" He turns to me and gives me a kiss on the forehead before his gray eyes find mine. "I should grab my shit and get going. I need to be at *Ravage* for an appointment soon."

"See ya later, man," Lucas says while pounding his fist with Alex's. "We'll be moving some of our stuff in over the weekend. I'm sure Tripp will fill you in on the rest of the details later. Cool?"

Alex nods his head and starts backing up. "Sure thing." He

turns back to me and winks. "Talk to ya later, Firecracker."

"I'll call you in a few hours," I say in response, ignoring his silly nickname for me.

Lucas watches as he walks down the stairs before turning back to me and pulling me against him. He presses his lips against mine and grips my ass in his hands. "You look so damn sexy wet. I hope you're in the mood, because I can't help myself right now."

He kisses me again before licking his lips and pulling away. "I told you he'd agree to move in. I just hope he doesn't mind us having a little fun once in a while. I'm not going to hold back just because he'll be living here too."

I let out a little breath and force a smile. "He'll be fine. I'm sure he'll have a ton of girls over anyways. He will hardly even notice."

Saying the words out loud only makes my heart ache.

"Yeah. Well who knows, maybe he will share with us. I don't mind sharing."

I let out a nervous laugh and try to hide the fact that for some reason that bothers me.

"Maybe," I whisper.

Maybe I want him all to myself . . .

THREE

ALEX

IT'S BEEN FIVE DAYS since Tripp asked me to move in with her and Lucas. I should have been moved in days ago, but the truth is my head is still reeling from our conversation at the bar. That and the fact that I have been extremely busy, working my ass off here at *Ravage*. I've been lucky to have any amount of free time in between my endless appointments.

"Hey dude. Alex," Ace calls out, probably from the gaming couch.

"Yeah, man?" I smile down at the sexy brunette in my chair as I hand her the mirror, allowing her to check out the dandelion I just placed below her right collarbone.

"Your girlfriend is here to see you," he replies with a hint of laughter. "She's looking damn fine too, so you better hurry your ass up." I hear him whisper, "Damn," as her footsteps start heading toward my door.

Everyone at the shop knows she's not my girlfriend, but after months of everyone calling her that, we have both given up on correcting them. It's not like it really bothers me anyways. If I were to ever have a girlfriend, Tripp would be the perfect one for the role; the only one able to capture my balls and lure me in, so fuck it.

Sliding my chair back, I look up to see Tripp appear in the doorway with a half-smile, dressed in another damn dress. *Fuck, those dresses do me in.* She glances down at the brunette that now seems to be glaring at me, looking jealous.

She gives me a knowing look. "Nice tattoo," Tripp confirms as the girl looks between Tripp and I, trying to get a read.

"Thanks," she says with a sneer, before looking at me. "I didn't realize you had a girlfriend." She stands from the chair and walks over to stand in front of me. "I've been hearing some things about you and I was *hoping* we could hang out sometime. I just assumed you were single from all the talk."

Before I can say anything, Tripp walks over to the chair and takes a seat, slapping the brunette on the ass. The girl seems surprised, but this chick never fails to surprise me. She's definitely something else. "He doesn't." She grabs the girl's arm and pulls her down so that her lips are close to the girl's ear. "And I can confirm that *everything* you've heard about this stud is true."

Tripp leans in closer, brushing her lips under her ear as the brunette lifts an eyebrow, her interest piqued once again. "Trust me," she whispers.

The brunette now looks back at me with a playful smile, looking hopeful once again. "I see," she says sweetly. "That's perfect."

"We're having a party tonight at our place," Tripp says proudly. "Ask Ace to hook you up with the address. It's not far from here."

"I'll definitely be there." She looks me up and down, admiring my body before saying, "The name is Mel by the way."

Tripp winks at me before smiling up at Mel. "We'll see you around eight, Mel. Don't keep my guy over here waiting for too long. The other girls will swoop in and take your place if they see the opportunity."

Mel looks a little nervous, before shaking it off and smiling. "Oh, I won't be late." She starts backing up toward the door while biting her bottom lip. "I'll see ya then, Alex."

Shaking my head, I look to Tripp and smirk as Mel turns around and exits the room. I somehow find what she just did to be extremely hot. "What was all that shit about?"

She shrugs her shoulders before reaching in her purse and pulling out a sandwich, tossing it to me. "I was just being your wingman . . . or would it be wingwoman?" She raises an eyebrow in thought, grinning from ear to ear.

I reply to her while unwrapping my ham and cheese sandwich and taking a bite. "You really are something else.

She would've came home with me no matter what. You know that, right?"

"Of course," she says in a high-pitched voice. "But I owe you for agreeing to move in with us. I had to make sure it was a done deal." She jumps up from the chair and wraps her arms around my neck. "I've been settled in for three days now. You need to hurry up and move in. I won't be excited until I see your stuff show up. I want you to call this place home. You promised me."

I run my hands up her arms before pulling them away and pushing her toward the door, pinning her up against it. I look her in the eyes so she can see the truth in them. "You know I'll be there. Just give me a few hours. I have two more appointments and then I'm out. I promise, Tripp. Never question that."

"Alright," she says with a nervous smile. She places her hands on my chest and looks down at them before looking back up at my face. "I'll be home setting up for the party. It's going to be a blast. I promise." She removes her hands and sucks her bottom lip into her mouth. "Later, Stud."

I smile at her and slap her ass as she turns around to leave. She lets out a small yelp and grabs her ass in surprise. I might have gotten a bit carried away and slapped it harder than planned. My bad.

"Ouch! That hurt." She punches my arm. "Jerk. Take your aggression out on someone else."

I back away and wink at her. "Just be glad it wasn't during sex. That hurts a lot worse. Trust me." I bite my bottom lip, as her face turns red. "Later, Firecracker." I tease.

She says nothing more before disappearing out the door, leaving me alone in my thoughts. Hearing Ace hit on her on the way out almost tests me, but I keep my shit together.

Control. It's all about control . . .

AFTER WORK I WENT BACK to the house, said goodbye to Memphis, and packed most of my shit into the back of my truck. It only took me about three hours to get everything moved and unpacked. By the time I was done, Tripp was standing in my doorway with a huge grin on her face, obviously glad that I kept my word.

"Someone looks awfully happy," I say while plopping down on my bed with my hands laced behind my head.

She runs across the room and jumps on the bed next to me, rolling on her side to face me, and propping herself up on her arm to look down at me. "Of course I am." She lays her head on my chest and throws her leg over my waist, tucking herself against my body. "My boy is finally here. I pretty much haven't seen you in five days. You know that is unacceptable. I've missed the shit out of you."

I close my eyes, feeling guilty for not at least stopping by to see her. I guess I have to admit that I've been a bit pissed off about her and Lucas being in the same house together. I just don't like the idea of her being around him every day. It feels too much like us.

"Well I'm here now." I sigh. "I won't let it happen again." I run my hand through the back of her hair and lightly tug on it. "Come here," I whisper.

She looks up at me before scooting up higher so that her face is tucked into my neck. *Damn, she smells so good.* "You promise me," she asks against my skin.

I grab her leg and pull her over me, positioning her so that she's partially lying between my legs, the rest of her body on top of me. Then I kiss her hair and tangle my fingers in it. We've been doing this since I was twelve. "Yeah. I just had to deal with a few things alone. You know I'm always here. If you would have asked me to come see you, you know there is no way in hell I could have said no."

"I know," she simply says. "I guess I just wanted you to come on your own."

I smile against her hair before grabbing her underneath her ass and pulling her up to straddle me. I rest my hands on the front of her thighs. "I come alone sometimes. A lot, actually." I laugh as she punches me and pushes down on my chest. She really doesn't realize that the way she's moving her body right now is about to give her a huge surprise if she doesn't hold still. "Would it be bad if I admitted I get hard when you punch me? I like it rough. Keep it up."

Her face turns red before she punches me a few more times. "Is that what I feel?"

She crawls off of me and rolls over on her back beside me on the mattress. "You really are a guy. I guess I should have found a girl for a best friend. Things would be a lot different."

I sit up and look at her while rolling my sleeves up to my elbows. "You have no idea."

She swallows, before breaking eye contact and standing, then walking toward the door. "So . . . you should get ready for the party tonight. I'm sure Mel will be showing up soon."

Having Mel here is the last thing I am even thinking about at the moment, but I guess having her around will keep me distracted from worrying about Tripp and Lucas and what kind of shit they'll be up to tonight. "Yeah. I'll be down in a bit. I'm going to relax and then take a quick shower. I've been up since five so I need to prep my brain for party mode."

Her eyes land on my guitar and she gives me a look, telling me she wants to hear me play it tonight. Then she backs out of my room and shuts the door behind her, leaving me alone in my thoughts.

I lay here for about an hour, lost in thought, before finally hopping in the shower and relieving myself. If it's a fucked up thing to stroke your cock to thoughts of your best friend, then I guess I'm extremely fucked up, but I have found this is the only way to be around her like I am on a near constant basis.

Standing under the warm water I stroke myself, slow and hard, to thoughts of me fucking Tripp so hard that she wouldn't be able to walk for weeks. Fuck me. The things I would do to her if I had a chance...

Gripping the shower wall, I stroke my cock a few more times, letting myself imagine that my hand is her pussy, before letting my cum wash down the drain, along with any ideas that being with Tripp would be okay. That shit will never happen without messing everything up.

I look down at my dick, while catching my breath and letting my orgasm wash through me as I slap the wall. Damn, that was a lot of cum. At least my dick won't be standing tall all fucking night now.

I guess we'll just see how the night plays out. Hell, maybe if I'm lucky I'll switch up Mel for Tripp. As shitty as that sounds, I want that so bad. The thought of her thighs squeezing me tight as I bury myself inside her has me getting hard again. I need to play it cool though. I have to. If I don't it could fuck up everything.

FOUR

TRIPP

I'M IN MY ROOM GETTING ready when I hear the shower turn on. The party starts in about fifteen minutes so Alex must be getting ready too.

Just out of curiosity, I walk over to the bathroom door and turn the handle. It moves, but I don't push it open. It's unlocked. That thought excites me, making me realize that he didn't care enough to lock it, and knowing that I could walk in at any time and see him naked elevates my core temp a little. I just find that to be so damn hot.

That's an open invitation . . . right?

I release the handle and suck in a small breath when I hear him moan out, followed by what sounds like his hand slapping against the shower wall.

SOMETHING FOR THE PAIN

Oh. My. God. That is the sexiest sound I have ever heard. That low, deep growl is all it takes to get me wet.

Collecting myself, I back away from the door and take a deep breath. My legs feel shaky. "Don't do this right now, Tripp. Dammit, don't do this." Shaking it off, I go back to stand in front of the mirror one last time, questioning the way I look in my newest little dress.

Dresses are my thing. It doesn't matter how many I own, I can never have enough. Plus, I love the way Alex looks at me every time he sees me in a new dress. His wandering eyes always cause my heart to flutter out of my chest. I just hope this little red dress is enough to get his attention.

I'm in the middle of turning around to check out my ass, when I hear the bathroom door open, followed by a whistle.

Please be naked . . . What am I saying? Don't be naked.

Cautiously, I turn my head toward the bathroom door, with my eyes squinted, to see Alex standing there in a towel. He looks so damn sexy that I feel as if all the air has been sucked from my lungs. My chest aches as I stare him up and down, watching as the water drips from his beautiful, tattooed body.

He checks me out with a smirk before whistling again. "Damn, Firecracker. That dress was made just for you." He places his hand over the bulge in his towel and bites his bottom lip. "You look beautiful. Stop second-guessing yourself. I'll see you downstairs in five."

He turns around, pulling the towel away right before he closes the door behind him. My mouth drops open from the glimpse of his ass that I am left with. It's so firm and perfect that all I can think about is biting it . . . and the way it flexed when he walked. Is it normal for an ass to look that good?

"I hate you sometimes," I whisper.

"Who do you hate sometimes?"

I shake my head and look at my doorway to see Lucas standing there, dressed in a black shirt and a pair of gray shorts. He raises his eyebrows, waiting for my response.

"No one." I walk over to him and plaster on my best smile, trying to pretend that I'm not still thinking about those sounds I heard coming from the shower. "I was talking to myself. Just second-guessing my outfit, I guess."

Wrapping his arms around me, he kisses my shoulder and brushes my hair behind my ear. "Well, I would have loved to see you in a pair of short shorts and a tank top tonight, but this dress works too."

I roll my eyes before pulling away from him and bumping him out of the way with my hip. "I didn't feel like wearing shorts, Lucas. This dress makes me feel good. If I feel good, then I have a good time and enjoy myself. That's all I want tonight."

"Me too, baby," he responds. "We're going to have a lot of fun. Trust me."

I start walking into the hallway, but feel his hand slide up my dress, slipping a finger inside of me. I stop right outside of my room and swallow. Closing my eyes, I begin imagining it were Alex.

"Holy shit, you are wet!" Wrapping his arm around my waist, he starts sliding his finger in and out, while moaning in my ear. "So damn wet. You've never been this wet before."

Opening my eyes, I look over to see Alex leaning against the wall next to his door, with his arms crossed over his chest. His eyes wander down to Lucas' hand and then up to meet my eyes.

Out of instinct I push Lucas away and pull my dress down to cover my ass back up. My heart is pounding like crazy. "Holy shit, Alex. I didn't know you were out here."

Lucas doesn't even seem to care that Alex just witnessed him fingering me. I bet he wouldn't be too happy to find out that Alex is the real reason I was already wet and not because of him.

He sucks his finger into his mouth and smiles at Alex. "Hey, man. People are arriving and there's some hot chick downstairs looking for you. I told her you were almost ready."

I can see the aggravation on Alex's face as he nods his head and walks past us. "Sure, man. Thanks."

My heart continues to race as I watch Alex quickly descend the stairs to be with a random chick that will get the one thing I have wanted for as long as I can remember, but unlike her, I can't have.

Clearing my throat, I tilt my head back as Lucas pushes me against the wall and kisses my neck. "Come on, Lucas," I say stiffly. "People are waiting on us." Not that I actually care. The truth is I don't really want to fuck Lucas after seeing the look on Alex's face. I have no idea what that look meant, but it was enough to make me want to forget it. He seemed bothered by our show.

Lucas spreads my legs open with his thigh, before running a hand up my leg and cupping my mound. "Shit, I'm so horny right now. Is it wrong that the thought of Alex watching me fuck you is turning me on? I might even like to watch him fuck you. Damn, baby."

I feel a surge of heat shoot through me and can feel the wetness dripping through my bikini bottom now. The thought of *Alex* and *fuck* in the same sentence makes it hard to think straight.

"Yeah," I whisper. "And do you think Alex would like that?" For some reason, I want to hear what he thinks about Alex. He's been around us enough to know more than anyone.

"Are you kidding me?" He pushes me harder against the wall and kisses my neck again, lost in his lust to have me. "Alex probably fantasizes about fucking you every day . . . about sticking his dick into your tight little pussy."

I moan out as he slips his finger back inside and slowly starts pumping. "Damn . . . so wet and so tight." He starts pumping faster and harder. "You want Alex to fuck you? Huh, baby? You want him to bust his load inside of you?"

I find myself moaning louder as I picture Alex inside of me.

"Maybe he can slide his hand up this dress later and finger fuck you just like I am. Do you think about doing that with your best friend? Huh? Do you imagine him pushing his fingers deep inside you? The same ones that he holds that tattoo gun with . . . You like that, huh? All the girls do." He speeds up again, going as deep as he can and I lose it. My whole body shakes from my orgasm and I have to grip onto Lucas' shirt to keep from falling.

"Oh fuck!" I try to keep quiet, but the orgasm just seems to keep rolling through me, shaking me to my core. "Damn you, Lucas! You just don't listen," I say breathlessly.

"Fuck. That was fast though, baby. You loved it."

I turn away and focus on catching my breath as the waves slowly begin to stop. He thinks that my orgasm was due to his abilities, but he couldn't be more wrong. If I didn't realize how much I wanted to have sex with Alex . . . well I do now. Lucas just helped confirm it.

"I'll meet you downstairs," Lucas says with a grin. "I know you need a minute to tidy up a bit first." Bringing his lips to mine, he kisses me softly, smiling against my lips, before hurrying down the stairs. Lucas is so into partying that I'll be lucky to see him the rest of the night now.

"Shit, shit, shit." I grip my hair and turn to face my door. My head is spinning. "I can't do this anymore. No more picturing Alex," I tell myself.

This is all hitting me so much harder now. Acting normal around Alex might be a little difficult after that. This is not cool, and definitely not what I expected. We haven't even lived together for a day yet.

Adjusting my dress, I go back into my room to change into a pair of panties. My bikini bottoms are so damn wet that they're bothersome; not to mention a huge reminder of how much Alex turns me on.

By the time I'm done pulling myself back together, I can

hear that the party has already started and the guests are starting to pile in. We invited over two hundred guests, so I have no doubt that it will be a hit.

Making my way downstairs, I smile at a few girls that I knew from high school and follow the rest of the party out back where the bar and DJ are set up.

I instantly spot Alex by the bar, getting a drink for himself and Mel. My stomach sinks as I watch him smile at her, as if he's enjoying her company. His smile is so damn sexy. I'm used to him being with girls, but I'm not used to witnessing it.

Handing her a cup, he wraps an arm around her tiny waist, before leaning in to whisper something in her ear. Her head tilts back as she laughs and bites her lip at whatever it is that he's saying.

Alex is good with women. He always has been, and that's another reason that I've kept my feelings to myself. There will always be someone out there that wants him. That's probably why he has never settled down; too many to choose from.

Just as I'm about to turn away and go look for Harley, Alex spots me, and his smile lights up. I see his eyes scan me before he mouths *Firecracker* at me. I shake my head at him and mouth *Stud* back at him.

He'll never stop teasing me with that damn name. I see him hold his finger up to Mel before he reaches for a glass and jogs over in my direction, leaving her alone by the bar. He stops right in front of me, holding his hand behind his back. "Everything okay?" He grabs my chin with his free hand and brings it up so he can look into my eyes. "You look like something's bothering you."

I grab his wrist and smile. "I'm fine, Alex. Why would you even think that?"

He scrunches his eyebrows at me and tilts his head. "I'm not stupid, Tripp. I've known you almost my whole life." He holds my hand up and tugs on the silver ring on my right ring finger. "You've been standing over here spinning your ring since you've stepped outside."

I look down at my ring and let out a frustrated breath before pulling my hand away. I hadn't even realized I was playing with it. I usually don't, since it comes so naturally. This ring is the only thing I have left of my parents. My mother left it behind when her and my father ran off when I was only seven. The same year I met Alex.

"I see you're very observational tonight," I mutter.

"I'm always observational," he says with a smirk. "I notice more than you know."

I feel my heart speed up as I watch his lips twitch. Why the hell am I so horny for him now? All I can think about is sucking his bottom lip into my mouth and biting it. *Damn you . . . and those sexy sounds from the shower.*

It's silent for a few seconds, both of us just looking at each other, before he speaks again.

"I see Lucas is already downing shots in the pool." He shakes his head before pulling a red cup out from behind his back and handing it to me. "One strawberry daiquiri, light on the rum. Drink up and enjoy yourself, but don't let Lucas feed you too many shots tonight. You always get sick." He points at the daiquiri. "That shit is special."

I can't help but to smile as he flashes me his dimples. "Thanks for the drink." I hold it up and take a long sip, surprised at how good it tastes. Everyone usually makes it too strong for me, but this . . . this is perfect, just how I like it. "Oh my god . . . this is so damn good, Alex." I take another drink, gripping onto his red and gray shirt with excitement. I needed this drink right now, and the taste is almost good enough to give me a mini orgasm.

"Better be." He grins and starts backing away. "I made that shit myself. Maybe I should become one of those shirtless bartenders on the side."

"Maybe." I laugh. "Thanks, Stud," I say teasingly.

"Oh you mean this stud?" He sticks his tongue out at me and waves it, showing off his new piercing. The way he moves his tongue so sexy and seductive, it's almost as if he's teasing me with what I'm missing out on.

Damn . . . he just had to add that to his sexiness.

"Put that tongue away before I bite it, Carter. I only need a few more of these to do it." I hold up my drink and smile.

Laughing, he waves his tongue one more time, before making his way over to Ace, who is now chatting with Mel. Alex stands to the side, chill, as if it doesn't bother him. Why should it? Alex doesn't have much competition anywhere he goes. If he wants to fuck you . . . he will, plain and simple.

I feel a slap on my shoulder, pulling me away from Alex. "Tripp. What the hell took you so long? I've been looking all over for you."

Turning beside me, I notice Harley standing there, wearing a long white dress with her bright pink bikini beneath it. Her long, blonde curls are pulled back into a ponytail and she's sporting a bright pink lip ring to match her bikini. Harley and I have been friends since we were both twelve. She's my only true female friend. All the other ones proved to be fake or too jealous over mine and Alex's friendship.

"Hey, sweets. Love the new ring." I reach out and gently tug on her lip ring as she laughs.

"Thanks, love." She takes a sip of her drink and eagerly looks around. "I've been waiting for Ace's sexy ass to show up. I had to make sure to see you first though so I didn't look like a shitty friend."

I give her a stupefied look. "Ace? Really, Harley? That guy can't keep his dick in his pants for longer than ten minutes."

She smirks at me and raises an eyebrow. "That's what I'm counting on. It's been six months since I caught Jason fucking Izzy and I've had a lot of frustration to take out. My hand's getting tired, honey."

I take a sip of my drink and nod behind her toward the bar, where Ace already has a few girls hanging close by. "Well you better hurry up before someone else snags his ass up. He's behind you at the bar, chatting it up with Alex and his date."

She hurries up and downs her drink, before wiping her mouth off. "Perfect timing. I'll be back. Just don't expect it to be anytime soon."

"Yeah," I say as she starts walking away. "Sure you will."

There's no way that girl is coming back. She's absolutely gorgeous and there's no way Ace will turn her down for someone else. Hell, I even kissed her one night when I was drunk. First time I had ever kissed a girl, and I have to admit that I definitely didn't dislike it.

I hear my name, followed by a whistle, so I turn behind me to see Lucas with a few of his guy friends chilling in the pool, along with about ten other random people partying it up. Must be friends of friends because I have never met any of these people.

"Over here, Tripp."

Smiling at him and his crazy friends that are now whistling at me and calling me over, I flip them all the middle finger and make my way over to them.

I stop in front of the pool and smile down at the guys, trying to decide if I want to get in or not. "Boys."

I jump back when Myles splashes me. "Hey, gorgeous." He looks me up and down and hits Lucas' shoulder. "Hot fucking dress. What's underneath?"

Placing my foot on his shoulder, I push him under the water before taking a seat on the edge of the pool and kicking him with some water to the face.

"Something you'll dream about later." I joke.

He places his hand to his scrawny chest. "Ouch! That hurt. Why can't I get in on some action?"

"Get in, baby." Lucas swims over right in front of me and

SOMETHING FOR THE PAIN

starts lifting my dress up my legs, not caring that all of his friends are eyeing me up. "Take this damn thing off and put that drink down."

I push his hand away and pull my dress back down my legs. "I'm not wearing my bikini yet. I'll get in later. We have all night."

He laughs as if I've just said something really stupid. "Your underwear is the same damn thing." He lifts his arms up and spins around. "Look around you. This is a party. No one gives a shit. You wanted to have fun. What are you waiting for? It's our first house party."

He goes to lift my dress up again, but I tug on it, still hesitant to strip down to my panties.

"Is there a problem?" Alex stops and asks on his way past. Releasing Mel's waist, he pushes his way through Lucas' friends and pulls me aside, his face not hiding his concern for me. "Tripp?"

I shake my head, feeling bad for the small scene. I never meant to get Alex worked up by thinking Lucas is a threat. "I'm fine." I pinch his cheek and smile. "Go have fun, Stud. We were just playing. I promise."

Alex turns from me to look over at Lucas and his friends. He takes a second to size them all up before turning back to me. "Better be." His jaw steels as his eyes meet mine. "Come find me if you need me."

"I always do," I say truthfully. "Better hurry before your date leaves."

He looks over his shoulder at Mel, nods his head, and

starts backing up. I see a small smile take over his face and I can't help but to full on grin at him.

Guess I'm going in the pool now. Tilting my drink back, I down the rest of it, before standing up. "Time to get wet." Without much thought, I rip my dress over my head, stripping down to my red bikini top and black panties.

I hear whistles coming from all directions before I dive into the pool, sinking to the bottom. The water feels so good; almost like an escape away from everything and everyone, at least for this short moment.

Relaxing under the water for a second, I grip onto my hair before pushing my way back up to the top.

Lucas immediately comes up behind me and pulls me into his arms. "Hand me that shot, dude."

One of his friends grabs for one of the shots lined up by the pool and hands it to him. Smiling, he holds it up to my lips. "You deserve this after all that hotness. Drink up."

Feeling a bit more relaxed now that I've already downed my first drink I part my lips and let him tilt the glass, allowing the liquid to run down my throat.

The DJ is playing music, people are getting wasted and having fun. This is exactly what I wanted - A little fun and freedom. Might as well live it up a little. A little celebration for having Alex here is how I view it. I couldn't ask for more.

IT'S GETTING DARK NOW, BUT everyone still seems to be

having the time of their lives. I haven't seen Alex much since before I got into the pool, but maybe that's because I've been trying to avoid seeing him with Mel. It makes my chest hurt too much. I really haven't seen much of Harley either, now that I think about it.

I'm probably up to my fifth drink and fourth shot by now. Once I get enough liquor inside of me, it becomes a little harder to say no. Especially when you're just having fun and trying to keep your head clear of certain unwanted thoughts.

I'm in the middle of everyone, just dancing and having a good time, and Lucas is surprisingly still beside me instead of off having fun. He shouts over the loud music and holds up two more shots before handing one of them to me.

I get ready to tilt it back, but I feel a hand reach out and snatch it away. It's Alex. It wouldn't be anyone else. Everyone else is too wasted to care about anyone else.

He steps in between Lucas and I and hands the shot back to Lucas. "She's done with shots, Lucas. Give that shit to someone else."

Before Lucas can say anything, Alex walks me out of the dancing crowd and over to the fire pit where it's a bit quieter. He pulls one of the chairs up behind me and helps me sit down.

I look up to see Lucas watching us, but then he just shrugs and hands the shot to a random guy close to him, going back into his party mode.

"I told you to be careful with shots, Tripp. I don't want to be cleaning puke off of you tonight. I will, trust me, but I'd rather not."

One look into his eyes and I can't argue with him. He always has a way of sobering me up. "I'm sorry," I whisper. I am too. I hate upsetting Alex.

"Don't be." He smiles and hands me a cup of water that Mel passes to him. "Drink this."

I can't help but to smile up at him. "I will if you do something for me."

He smiles. "You know I'll do whatever, Tripp. Don't I always?"

I nod my head. "Play your guitar for us," I whisper. "Please. Please. Please."

His lips turn up into a smile, but he doesn't respond. He looks around the crowd full of people, before bringing his attention back to me.

"Please. It will help relax me."

He lets out a huff. "You're so damn lucky that I can't say no to you. You have no idea." He turns to Mel. "I'll be back."

Mel looks at me, and smiles awkwardly, but doesn't say a word. She almost looks . . . jealous. *Of me? Ha! That's funny.*

Alex is inside for about ten minutes before I notice him come back outside. Everyone clears a path for Alex, as he walks confidently with his guitar. He doesn't seem to have a care in the world. He's about to own this party and he knows it. I know it. He's owned me for years with that guitar.

Something about his confidence has always drawn me to him, making me want him way more than I should, and seeing all these people waiting for him to sing for us makes me want him that much more. It's almost unbearable.

He stops once he gets back to the fire pit and smiles as he throws the strap of his guitar over his head. Almost everyone is now looking at him, and the DJ has stopped the music. "You asked for it." He works on adjusting the strings of his guitar, while still talking. "I'm playing this song, because let's face it, all you fuckers are having sex after you leave this party."

Everyone starts screaming and cheering him on, but his face stays focused as he starts playing the melody to a song that I recognize right away: *Wicked Games* by The Weeknd. If people weren't planning on fucking after this party . . . well they will be now.

A few girls, including Mel, start dancing close to Alex as the seductive words leave his lips. *Holy shit . . . that voice.* It's been a while since I've heard him sing.

Closing my eyes, I get lost in his words, imagining his lips running across my skin with each word; the vibration of his voice against my flesh as he touches me in all the right places. Oh the things he can probably do with his mouth.

Maybe being drunk isn't helping liked I'd hoped . . .

Before I know it, I'm standing just a few steps away from Alex, hanging on his every word. His eyes meet mine as he sings.

My eyes stay locked with his, unable to pull away. There's something in his eyes right now that almost makes it feel as if he's truly singing those words to me. It feels like just the two of us.

I feel my body shuddering with each word that leaves his sexy as sin mouth, as he gets deeper into the song and the melody picks up.

While still singing, he swings the guitar around his body so that it's now hanging from his back. Reaching out, he pulls me against his body as he grinds his hips against me and sings.

Letting out a small breath, I spin around in his arms and lean my head against his shoulder as I let myself dance against him. I feel his lips against my ear as he continues the song, seductively running his hands up the length of my arms as I hold them out at my sides.

Then, before I know it, he's gone and reaching for his guitar again. I stop dancing for a second, but he nods his head at me, encouraging me to keep going.

A few seconds later I feel another set of arms wrap around me, and I know right away that it's Lucas. He starts dancing against me, but his movements aren't in sync with mine. Not like Alex's were.

Knowing that I need to get my mind somewhere else, I dance with Lucas, hoping that feeling him against me will bring my thoughts to him.

"You look so sexy when you dance," he whispers in my ear.

I feel myself leaning into him as we both dance to the sound of Alex's voice, but as soon as the song finishes, I suddenly start to feel really anxious, as if I need to get away for a minute.

I turn around in his arms and place my hands to his chest. "I'm not feeling so hot right now. I think I need to go inside for a minute."

"Alright." Lucas takes a swig of his beer before kissing my forehead. "Come back when you're feeling better. I'm going to keep our guests busy."

My eyes pull away and meet Alex's before I push my way through the crowd and break through the silence of the back door.

Once I get inside, I walk over to the stairs and take a seat half way up the steps. Closing my eyes, I lean my head against the wall and let out a deep breath.

My thoughts are really messing with me right now. I'm starting to wonder if asking Alex to move in was good for any of us. I can't seem to keep my eyes off of him long enough to think straight.

"You feeling okay, babe?"

I look up to the sound of Alex's voice. He's standing at the bottom of the stairs with his guitar in hand. My heart swells at the sight of him.

"I'm fine." I watch him with a smile as he walks up the steps and sits down next to me. "You should be out there enjoying the party and not in here worrying about my ass. I'm sure Mel is waiting on you."

He bites his bottom lip in a teasing manner. "Oh, I'm always thinking about your ass . . . and Mel can wait."

Blushing, I push his shoulder.

His face turns serious. "No, for real though . . . I can't

enjoy myself knowing that my favorite girl isn't feeling well."

I look up and smile at him as he reaches for my hand and helps me to my feet. "Come on. Let me get you to bed."

Walking in front of him, I rest my head on his chest as he grabs my hips and guides me up the stairs. I feel a bit wobbly. "You're the best friend a girl could ask for. You know that, right?" My words slur a little, but I hope he knows how much I mean them.

He pushes my bedroom door open and takes a seat in my chair as I plop down onto my bed.

"I know," he says softly. Without me even asking, he starts playing his guitar as I close my eyes and eventually dose off.

FIVE

ALEX

I'VE BEEN UP FOR THE last two hours. Actually—I barely even slept at all. I've never been one for sleeping much, so there's nothing new there, but I have a feeling that last night had something to do with my lack of sleep this time. I couldn't help but notice Lucas make his way into Tripp's room late last night. The little noises that she made while he pounded into her will forever haunt my dick now. He was in there for twelve minutes before I heard him leave again. Yeah, that's right . . . I timed it. Something about knowing that he fucked her just a room over from me didn't settle well with me last night, and I couldn't seem to shut my mind off. Especially since he couldn't even be man enough to take care of her when she needed it. That just pisses me off.

The party ended for me earlier than I expected last night. After Tripp got sick and I put her to bed, I returned my guitar to my room and went back outside to join the party. No matter how hard I tried, I just couldn't seem to get my head back into partying like everyone else. A huge part of me felt like I should've been lying in bed with Tripp, holding her. Except . . . that's not my place. It's someone else's. So I didn't.

Instead, I tried my best to focus my attention on Mel, who wanted nothing more than to hang all over my nuts. Especially after she heard me playing my guitar for everyone. She said it was the sexiest thing she had ever seen a man do. I knew she wanted to fuck, so that's what I gave her. I took her to the downstairs shower, banged her until she couldn't walk, and then sent her on her way.

That's how things always work with me and women. I meet them at the tattoo shop, take them home, fuck them, and move onto the next. It's been that way for six months now. You might call me a prick, but I never promise these women anything. They want to be fucked, so that's what I give them. Nothing more.

I've been running for the past fifty minutes now; sweat pouring down my bare chest as I let out a bit of frustration. It's hot as balls out here, but I haven't been able to force myself to stop. I won't stop until I'm out of breath and my legs give out on me, just like with sex.

Ever since I stopped fighting, this has been my release. It feels good to just run and never stop. It's freeing.

I've already passed the house—our house—three times now. And every time I do, I can't help but to stop and look up at Tripp's window to see if she's awake yet. I want to know if Lucas is back in her bed. As fucked up as it sounds, I want to drag his ass out of it.

Running to the back of the house, I open the large gate and let myself into the yard. I start stripping myself of my shorts and boxer briefs as soon as the pool comes into view. Taking a long, deep breath, I dive into the deep water and relax, letting myself sink to the bottom before swimming back up to the surface.

The cool water feels good on my heated flesh, but it does nothing to calm my thoughts of Tripp.

I need to push these fucked up thoughts aside. It's messing with everything. *Tripp. Naked. In my bed. Me fucking her. Hard. So damn hard.*

I swim for at least thirty minutes, trying to clear my head, before climbing out of the water and reaching for my boxer briefs. Without bothering to get dressed, I just cover my junk up with my boxers and let myself in through the back door.

Everyone should still be asleep anyways. When I walk into the kitchen, I'm surprised to see Lucas standing at the bar with a cup of coffee in hand. Guess I was wrong.

He holds up his mug and smiles lazily at me, while glancing down at the small piece of fabric covering my dick. "Someone's up early."

I nod my head. "Yeah. I don't sleep much."

I'm standing here dripping wet and naked, but Lucas doesn't act as if it bothers him. Part of that makes me want to say fuck it and just run around naked all the time. If he doesn't care if Tripp sees me naked . . . then I sure as hell don't.

Walking over, he holds his fist out for me to bump it. "Someone got a good fucking in the shower last night. Damn that girl can scream. I can see why you had to cool off in the pool."

I smirk, but don't say anything as I reach into the fridge for a bottle of water.

"Shit man, I had to go upstairs and get mine in after that. I seriously don't think I've ever fucked Tripp so fast and hard in my life. I had to cover her mouth just to keep from waking you up."

I feel my stomach sink and anger build up inside, but I push it aside and pretend that his words don't bother me. Tripp is a grown woman now. I need to remember that.

I tilt back the water and down the whole bottle as he continues to talk.

"That pussy is tight, man. So damn tight. And talking dirty to her had her soaking wet. That girl is special." He pauses for a second to moan at his memories. "Well, I need to be at the bank in twenty minutes, so I need to take off. Tell Tripp I'm off at one, will ya?"

I nod my head as I toss the empty water bottle down and grip onto the sink, letting my briefs hit the floor. "Yup. Not a problem."

I wait for his footsteps to retreat before I look up again. I stand by the sink for a few more minutes before I reach for my briefs and pull them up over my now dry body.

"Fuck. What the hell is my problem?" I run my hands through my wet hair before digging through the fridge in search of eggs and strawberries.

Trying to block out everything that just came out of Lucas' mouth, I cook up some French toast and scrambled eggs, topping the toast off with a little powdered sugar and fresh strawberries. Then I quickly pour a glass of orange juice before making my way upstairs.

Thanks a lot, Lucas. *Don't think about her pussy . . . This is so messed up.*

TRIPP

I HEAR MY DOOR PUSH open, but I'm too tired to acknowledge it. It can't be any later than seven thirty in the morning, so I just stay lying on my stomach.

I hear something get set down on my computer desk before I feel the bed dip down next to me. It must be Lucas saying goodbye before he has to get ready for work.

Groaning, I reach out and grip his upper thigh, surprised at how hard and thick it feels in my hand. I guess I never really paid his legs much attention before. "Ughhhh . . . my head. Why did you give me all those shots last night? I feel like hell?" I run my hand up higher, stopping just below his package. Why does he feel so good right now?

"You look like hell too," Alex says playfully.

Shocked, I let go of his thigh and grip onto the sheet to cover my bare breasts, while maneuvering my way to my knees. I almost forgot that Alex finally moved his stuff in last night. Man, I really must've had a few too many shots.

"Crap, Alex. I thought you were Lucas." I reach up with one hand to cover my face as my head starts pounding. "I guess I drank a little too much last night." I pull my hand away and squint from the light shining in my room. "I almost grabbed your dick, Alex. You weren't even going to say anything?"

Grinning, Alex stands up, and I can't help but to notice how sexy he looks, wearing only a tight pair of boxer briefs. Not only do I get him as a roommate, but now I'll also have to see him running around in his underwear. Talk about a distraction.

"Just a few too many." He runs his hand through his wet hair. "And I'm not going to stop something that feels good. I'm sure your hand was enjoying it too much. Now sit up straight."

I watch as Alex walks over to my desk and grabs a plate and a glass of something. My head hurts too much to even pay attention to his words. "What's this?" I ask as he sets the plate on my lap. "You made me breakfast?"

He sets the glass down on the nightstand beside me and I peek over to see that it's orange juice. "Yeah." Without another word, he walks into the bathroom. I almost think he's going back to his room, until he emerges a few seconds later, holding something in his hand. He places two pills into my hand and crosses his arms over his chest. "Ibuprofen. Take those and eat your food."

Not questioning him, I do as told. The first bite of food causes me to smile at its deliciousness. "Oh my goodness, Alex." I point down at the toast before taking another bite and quickly chewing it. "This is absolutely delicious. Wow."

He smiles. "Tell me something I don't know."

I toss a piece of egg at his head. "Cocky much?" I laugh as he grabs my hand and takes a bite of the eggs that I was just about to eat. "Very much so." He chews the eggs and rubs a hand over his stiff abs. "What you doing before work?"

"I was going to stop by and visit Tara. You want to come with?"

He nods his head and starts backing away to the bathroom. "Yeah. I'm sure she misses the shit out of me."

I laugh, accidently spitting the mouthful of toast out. "Seriously?" I cover my mouth and smile. "It's only been like a week. Trust me, she does not miss you."

He flashes me his dimples. "We'll see about that." He gets ready to walk out of my room, but stops and grabs onto the frame. "Oh and Lucas left for work already. He said he'll see you around one."

Figures he wouldn't say bye. "Alright . . . thanks." I take a sip of my orange juice. "I'll shower after I eat and then we can go. Sound good?"

"Everything out of your mouth sounds good." He attempts to catch the egg in his mouth as I throw it at him. "You have a horrible aim. I'm going to go downstairs and work out for about twenty minutes and then take a quick shower. I'll shower downstairs so I don't slow you down."

Eyeing his body up and down, I swallow, remembering the dirty sounds coming from the downstairs shower last night. I tried so hard to block them out, but it was pretty hard to miss. I have to admit that hearing Alex fuck, both turned me on and bothered me at the same time. A part of me wanted to imagine myself taking her place, while the other part wanted to pretend that I wasn't imagining it at all.

Then Lucas came up here saying dirty things to me about Alex . . . once again, turning me on so bad that I practically knocked him down and jumped on his dick. We had wild, meaningless sex, and then I sent him down to his room. Sleeping in the same bed as Lucas is something that I haven't done yet. I've only slept next to Alex, and for some reason . . . I want to keep it that way for now.

"Sounds good. We can take your truck." I smile while taking another bite of food.

"You just can't get enough of my awesome driving, can you? You like it fast and wild." He winks. "I like that."

I point my fork at him. "Just hurry up so we can get going."

"Sure thing, babe." He dodges out of my room, leaving me grinning from ear to ear. He always has a way of making me smile. I honestly don't know what I would do without him.

After I finish with breakfast and down the pills that Alex gave me, I start searching through my closet for fresh clothes to wear. Settling on a pair of old jeans and a black tank top, I throw my clothes down onto the bathroom rack and listen for the shower downstairs.

I can't tell if he's already inside yet, so I throw on the first shirt that I see and run downstairs to see if he's still working out. I just remembered that I have the early shift at the bar today so we really don't have a lot of time to waste.

By the time I get to the rec room, Alex is standing up beside the huge weight bench, wiping sweat from his face. My eyes trail down, following the beads of sweat dripping down his heaving chest, wetting the front of his tight briefs. My breath catches in my throat as I notice the shape of his dick moving beneath the fabric with the rhythm of his heavy breathing.

He notices me standing here and smiles as he pulls the towel away. "I'm getting in the shower now. Am I holding you up?"

I watch as every muscle in his body flexes to his movements as he reaches up to dry his hair with the towel. Shaking my head, I respond. "No. I was just making sure you were about to jump in the shower. I only have two hours before I need to leave for the bar."

He tosses his towel aside and walks over to me, throwing me over his sweaty shoulder. He walks us out of the room, down the hall, and sets me down at the bottom of the steps.

"Well then, we better hurry up." He turns around to walk away and my eyes land directly on his firm ass. "Meet me by my truck in twenty minutes."

Mmm . . . so perfect. Too perfect . . .

"Alright." I jog up the stairs and quickly strip myself in my room before closing myself into the bathroom and turning on the shower water. I shake my head, trying to clear it. Living with Alex is just too damn much.

I'm going to be in a world of trouble with this boy . . .

SIX

TRIPP

TWENTY MINUTES LATER, I'M FOLLOWING Alex outside and to his truck. He opens the door for me and grips the back of my thighs, boosting me into the seat. "Hold on, Firecracker." He winks and shuts the door, before jogging around the truck and to the driver's side.

Turning to me, he notices that my seatbelt isn't on, so he reaches over and secures it before slamming his door shut and buckling his own. "You know . . . I think I can manage to put on my own seatbelt."

He laughs while turning the key in the ignition and shifting the truck into reverse. He turns to me. "Nah, you definitely can't handle that." He starts backing out of the driveway while still talking. "Don't think that I haven't taken notes of the times I've seen you driving without a seatbelt. That shit won't happen on my watch, Tripp."

Turning red, I look away, embarrassed. I sometimes forget when I'm in a hurry, but I hadn't thought that anyone else noticed. That's just another reason that Alex will feel the need to take care of me now. I hate making him feel that way.

"I'll make sure I buckle up every time I get in a vehicle, okay?" I turn back to him as he concentrates on the road. "You don't need to worry about me."

"I try not to," he mumbles. "But I find it hard as shit."

I know that feeling well, because I feel the same way about him.

When we arrive at Tara's, me and Alex jump out at the exact same time and meet at the front of his truck. He places his hand on my lower back as we walk to the door.

Tara is standing by the TV on her tippy toes, attempting to hang a picture when she notices our entry. "Tripp." She inches a little higher, still struggling to get it hung. "Glad you're here. How about some help?"

I hear Alex chuckle before walking up behind her and helping her hang it and straighten it. "Good thing she brought a man along," Alex says.

Tara turns around and greets Alex with a warm smile. "And I was starting to miss this man." She squeezes his arm teasingly. "These muscles come in handy."

Alex flashes me his dimpled smile. "Told you," he says in a cocky tone.

I throw my arms up. "Yeah, yeah, yeah. You win. Apparently everyone misses you when you're away."

Laughing, Tara walks over to give me a hug and a kiss on the cheek. "Jealous much? Don't worry . . ." She pinches my cheek. "I missed you too." She turns away and whispers to Alex. "Not as much as I missed you though."

Nudging her with my arm, I move past her and make my way into the kitchen. "Did you make my favorite brownies? I need a stash for work today."

I start looking through her cupboards, not finding what I'm in search of. Then out of the corner of my eye, I see Tara open the oven and pull out something wrapped in foil.

"Oh calm down. You know I always have some ready for you when you ask." She tosses the brownies to me and reaches to pour herself a glass of wine. "You're just lucky I was in the baking mood last night and that I was bored out of my mind."

Tara was only twenty when my parents disappeared, leaving her to watch over me. She wasted all of her young adult life raising me as her own and I can never be more thankful to her. I owe her so much. She just turned thirty-three a few weeks ago, but she doesn't act a day over my age. I guess she's making up now for all her lost years.

Not even two seconds after Alex walks into the kitchen, Whisper—the cat that Alex gave me when I was fifteen—runs up to Alex's leg and digs her claws in, asking to be picked up.

I swear that cat is in love with him. Even though *I* raised her, she always clings onto Alex whenever he's around. I find it to be adorable and sickening at the same time.

Without hesitation, Alex picks Whisper up, burying his face into her fluffy, white fur while rubbing under her chin. "Hey girl. You missed me too, huh?"

I roll my eyes, but laugh to myself. I love seeing Alex so happy and full of love. He's in a much better place than he was over six months ago, before his brother Memphis returned. I wouldn't trade seeing Alex happy for anything else in the world. He deserves it more than anyone.

He's been through more pain and suffering than anyone I know and he's still open to happiness, always thinking of others first. I, on the other hand, get abandoned by my parents and can't even manage to let anyone in. Well, besides Tara and Alex. Trusting just doesn't come easy to me. That's why Lucas and I have the arrangement that we do.

It's worked well so far . . . I guess we'll see if we can make it past this year mark.

"How's the living arrangements working out," Tara asks while sipping on her wine. "Must be nice living with two guys. I really need to find myself one of those."

I laugh while shoving the brownies into my purse. "It's fine. Too bad you missed our party last night. There were plenty of hot guys there. You just need to get out more."

"Had to work. I always have to work. It doesn't leave me much time to go looking for dates at a party." She turns to Alex. "Don't you have an older brother or something?"

Alex gives her a little smile. "You're a little late on that. He's taken now."

"Well shit." Tara refills her wine glass. "Oh well. I'll find me a hunk sooner or later. I get a vacation in a few weeks. Maybe you two can hook me up." She raises an eyebrow. "As long as he's over the age of twenty-five and looks half as good as Alex, I'll be happy. Oh and he has to have a job too. I won't be anyone's sugar mama."

Alex flashes his dimples, but doesn't say a word while he pets Whisper.

"I'll get right on that." I tease.

We hang out with Tara for the next hour, talking and having a good time before saying our goodbyes and heading back to the house.

I have to be at work in less than twenty minutes now, so I need to be able to grab my apron and throw my hair up.

Alex stops at the bottom of the staircase, yelling up at me as I dash into my room. "I'm going to be at the parlor until around six. How about I just drop you off and then I can meet you at *Dax's* when I get off?"

Dax is the newest bar here in *Crooked Creek*. It opened up about four months ago and Dax, the owner, asked me if I wanted to start out as a cocktail waitress and work my way up to bartending. It seemed like a fun time, so I said yes. I love getting to interact with the customers, and just have a good time so it seemed perfect.

"Yeah, sure." I scream down to him while tossing my hair into a loose bun. "I'll meet you at your truck in five. I just need to find my . . . "

I look up at my doorway from shuffling through the pile

of clothes on my floor, to see Alex holding my apron. "This? I saw it laying in the bathroom last night, so I threw it in the washer with my clothes this morning." He tilts his head to the side. "Let's go. My truck's running and ready to go."

Grateful, I jump back to my feet and grab my apron out of his hand. "Always thinking ahead. You're too damn good to be true, Alex." I throw an arm around his neck, in a quick hug, before jogging down the stairs. I need to be at the bar in time to do all of the opening procedures and we're really starting to push for time. The night waitresses never leave the station stocked, so I end up spending most of the time refilling sauces and crap.

I beat Alex out to his truck and quickly hop in, buckling my seatbelt before Alex can say anything. He hops in about two seconds behind me and quickly backs out of the driveway.

He groans when we pull up at the bar to see Dax leaning against his black Mercedes, most likely waiting on me. "What a fucking douche."

"He's not that bad, Alex." I lean over and plant a quick kiss on Alex's cheek. "I'll see you later. Stop worrying about Dax, and thanks for the ride."

I hop out and slam the door, right as Alex mumbles bye back. He waits until Dax and I are walking in the door before taking off and heading to the tattoo shop.

Overprotective much?

Dax raises an eyebrow, while flipping on the light switches. "I guess your boyfriend is worried I'll make a move on you?"

I shake my head and walk past him. "We've already had this discussion. He's not my boyfriend." I laugh and set my purse down. "But yes. He probably thinks you're going to make a move. He's just really protective of me, and for some reason . . . he doesn't like you."

"Yeah, well if you ask me, he might as well be your boyfriend." He opens the door to his office and stops to look back at me. "He already acts like it anyways. And by the way . . . if I knew that you wanted me to, I would."

"Good to know." I tease. "You would know if I wanted it, but I'm good."

"Alright. Just pointing it out," he says teasingly. "Let's get things ready and fast. I have a feeling that we'll have an early rush today."

Without another word he disappears into his office, leaving me to set up the waitress station.

My boyfriend. Alex as my boyfriend.

My heart skips a beat at the thought.

If only it were that easy . . .

SEVEN

ALEX

I'M SITTING IN MY ROOM at the shop, cleaning off my equipment, when I hear someone clear their throat from the doorway. It doesn't even take me looking to know who it is. I've heard that annoying sound for far too many years of my life.

I smile from my seat, but don't bother looking up. "Memphis . . . what's up, big bro? Miss me already?"

I hear his footsteps as he enters the room, stopping behind me. "Fuck no." He squeezes my shoulder, causing me to look up from my cleaning. "Lyric is busy at the studio, so she asked me to stop in and check on you."

I can't help but to grin. "So *she* misses me . . . is what you're getting at?"

He slaps me on the back of the head before taking a seat in the other chair. "Surprisingly so." He flashes me a smile, before getting serious. "I suppose I do too. It's going to take a while before I can trust that you won't just fucking take off somewhere."

"I'm not going anywhere, man. Chill."

It's silent for a few moments as I finish putting my things away, before Memphis speaks again. "You been staying away from the alley?"

Standing up, I look down at him while leaning against the table. "I've stopped in to watch a couple fights. That's it. Nothing big." I nod my head toward the door, letting Memphis know that I'm ready to get going. It's been a long, stressful day, and all I can think about is relaxing with a nice, cold beer.

He stands up and follows me to the door. "Have you been to any of Trevor's fights?"

"Yeah. I caught the end of one a couple nights ago. He's getting pretty damn good. Won by KO."

"Yeah," Memphis says. "Maybe we'll have to stop by one night and watch a few fights for old time sakes. As long as we're both on the outside of that ring, that's all that matters to me. We don't belong there anymore. Don't forget that."

I nod my head while locking my door behind us. It's been over six months since either of us has been in a ring. I'm not trying to go back to that shit.

I slap the front desk. "I'm out, Styles."

Without looking up, Styles mumbles something as we

walk past and outside.

Memphis turns to me and grips my shoulder. "I'll tell Lyric that you're doing fine and that you're just as annoying as ever."

"That's my best quality, brother." I walk backwards, giving Memphis the middle finger with both hands, before jumping into my truck and starting the engine.

He stands there and watches me the whole time that I back out and pull off.

He's exactly who I got my protective nature from, and just like me . . . he never backs down.

I pull up at *Dax's* a little earlier than expected. Tripp still has about thirty minutes left before she gets off, but I decided to just show up early and kick back with a few beers while waiting. I could use a little unwinding before heading back to the house and seeing her and Lucas together.

The bar is pretty packed when I walk in, but I easily spot Tripp over at one of the tables close to the bar. It's a pretty full table, so not wanting to add to her pressure I make my way up to the bar to order a beer. I smirk at Harley as she looks up at me from wiping down the sticky mess in front of her.

"Harley. Just the girl I'm looking for."

Harley smiles from ear to ear and her face instantly turns red. Of course she knows that I know. Ace can't keep his mouth shut for crap. "Don't even say it, Carter." She points at me as she reaches below her for a beer, already knowing what I'm after.

I shrug my shoulders, trying to hide my grin. "I wasn't going to say shit about you and Ace fucking. I promise." I laugh and she tosses the beer cap at me, hitting me on the nose.

"Alex! I want to strangle you sometimes." She leans over the bar, suddenly interested, looking around to see if anyone's listening. "Tell me what he said. Don't leave anything out or I'll choke you."

Standing up, I grab the bottle of beer and lift it up, chuckling under my breath. I love screwing with her. "Cheers, Harley. I'll see you later." I walk backwards, smiling while tilting back my beer.

"You dick!" Harley shakes her head while giving me the evil eye. "I'll get it out of Tripp. Trust me."

Tripp appears beside me out of nowhere, so I wrap my arm around her neck and pull her to me. "No you won't. Tripp doesn't tell anything that I ask her not to."

Harley bites her bottom lip in annoyance. "True . . . and I hate you for that." She slaps her towel down onto the bar before crossing her arms. "Dammit! Fucking men! What are they good for?" She tilts her head in thought. "Oh yeah. Well double damn."

Turning around, I pull Tripp with me as I find an empty seat away from all the noise and Harley's man-hating ass right now. "Hey, babe." I kiss her forehead before sliding into a booth. "How's work?"

She rolls her eyes and lets out a frustrated breath. "Oh you know . . . busy as shit. And for some reason, Dax has only me on the schedule for another thirty minutes." She holds up three fingers. "Then he has three girls coming in. He expects me to hold the joint down by myself, but can schedule three girls for the late shift. He's lucky he left over two hours ago or I'd be choking him in a corner somewhere."

Getting lost in how damn cute she looks when she's mad, I let my teasing come out, unable to stop myself. I might just get punched for this, but it's always well worth it. "I'd let you choke me in the corner. Anytime and anywhere." I take a swig of my beer, before setting it down. "As long as it involves rough, dirty sex afterwards."

Her face flushes red, but she doesn't say anything, because some people from a few tables over start yelling her name annoyingly, trying to get her attention. "You're so damn lucky, slick." She pinches my nipple, hard, and then walks away, leaving me with a near hard-on.

She's lucky, because if she did that when we were alone, then I'd have a really hard time not bending her over and fucking her. Best friend or not.

I'm trying to keep my thoughts in check, but I can't when she does things like that to me.

I'm sitting alone for about five minutes, just enjoying my beer, when a petite blonde scoots into the booth across from me. She's cute, but I'm not interested in more than a short conversation. My head is somewhere else.

She holds out her hand and smiles. "Mandy."

Flashing her my dimples, I reach for her hand and shake it in mine. "Alex." I nod down at her drink when I notice that it's close to empty. "Let me buy you another drink."

Tripp walks past just as I'm about to get up and go to the bar, so I grab her wrist to stop her. She looks down at me about to say something, but stops when she notices the blonde sitting across from me. She stiffens for a second, before clearing her throat and smiling. "Hey."

"Mandy . . . this is my good friend, Tripp. She's also the sexiest waitress I've ever seen." I wink at Tripp with a smile, hoping to ease the tension.

Mandy flashes a small smile before reaching for her hand and shaking it. "Nice to meet you, Tripp. My name is Mandy."

"Mandy." She nods her head. "Let me get you two some new drinks. What will it be?"

I grip Tripp's waist and squeeze it. "You don't have to do that. I'll just go up to the bar."

Tripp looks down at me and pinches my arm. "Why are you so stubborn? This is my job, Alex. I can manage to get you some drinks."

Before I can say anything, Mandy holds up her glass, interrupting us. "A Vodka and lemonade will be good."

Tripp smiles at me and starts backing away. "One Vodka Lemonade and Miller Lite coming right up." She spins on her heels and walks away, and I can't help but to feel my stomach sink.

The idea of her waiting on me and some chick makes me feel oddly sick to my stomach. I barely like her waiting on me. It just doesn't feel right. I like to be the one waiting on her . . . always.

I make light talk with Mandy, trying not to lead her on too much, while waiting for Tripp to return with our drinks. I look over to see her and Harley discussing something at the bar as Harley glances our way, but I can't really get a read on Harley's expression. She usually looks irritated, so it's hard to tell.

Harley slides two drinks across the bar and then Tripp quickly grabs them and starts making her way back to us.

I have the urge to go to her and snatch the drinks before she can serve us, but she gives me that look. The one that will surly make me lose control and rip her clothes off in a corner somewhere if I fight her on it for too long.

"It's on the house, along with your first beer too, Alex, and don't even think about trying to fight it." She sets the drinks down. "I'm going to close out my tabs and I'll be ready soon."

She begins to walk away, but I stop her. There's no way I'm leaving this bar without paying. She knows how much I hate that. "I'm paying for the drinks and I'll fight it all I fucking want. That's what I do." I pull out a twenty and two tens, and then hand them to her. "I don't want any change either. You two split it."

She tries protesting, but I send her on her way with a slap to the ass. She glowers at me, before walking away and yanking her apron off.

Mandy stands up and gives me an uncomfortable look. "I'm sorry. I didn't realize that you had a girlfriend. I knew you were too gorgeous to be single." She holds up her drink. "Thanks for the drink. I can pay you back if you'd like."

I smile up at her and reach for my beer. "She's my best friend." I take a swig. "And it's not a problem."

She hesitates for a moment before speaking again. "It looks a lot to me like something more is going on."

"There isn't," I reply simply.

Looking me up and down, she reaches into her bag and pulls out a pen. "Well I have some friends over there." She points over to a table close by, occupied by three girls that suck at hiding their girly chatter and excitement for their girl, Mandy. "And I'm pretty sure you're about to leave anyways. Can I give you my number?"

I tell her like it is, just like I do all the other women. "I know this sounds shitty, but I'm more of a one night type of guy. I'm just not looking for anything else. So if you're okay with just having a good time . . ." I tilt back my beer before setting it down in front of me. "Then you can leave your number. I'm not trying to get mixed up in anything that I'm not ready for."

She bites her bottom lip in thought, before reaching for a napkin and scribbling down her number. She slides it across the table with a grin. "I'd take anything I could get from a guy like you. Sometimes that's all us women need." She stands up straight and starts backing away. "Call me anytime . . . Alex."

I grab her number and nod my head as she turns and walks away, joining her table of girlfriends. Then, I turn back to my drink and quickly finish it off before checking on Tripp to see if she's ready.

She grabs my arm and starts pulling me toward the door so fast that she almost trips on the way out. "I need to get out of here, Alex. What the hell was Dax thinking?"

I shrug while holding the door open for her. "Told you he's an idiot. I never lie to you, babe."

She laughs under her breath, but doesn't look back at me. "Sticking with the M's, I see."

"Only this week."

I open my truck door for her, but she just looks at me and lets out a frustrated breath. She looks as if she has something to say, but stops herself. I don't like her doing that. "Say it, Tripp." Grabbing the top of the truck, I pin her against it and look into her eyes, waiting for her to speak.

Nothing. She just shakes her head and smiles weakly. "I'm just tired and frustrated. I want to give Dax a piece of my mind." Maneuvering her way past my arm, she jumps into my truck and shuts the door. Moments later she pokes her head out the window. "Any day now, Carter," she says teasingly.

Tell me about it . . .

I SIT IN MY ROOM FOR a bit, playing my guitar. It's close to midnight and Tripp and Lucas have been downstairs, drinking and laughing it up. A part of me wants to join in, but the other part is too exhausted to pretend that I don't want to have my way with her.

That's all I've been able to think about since moving in the other day . . . and the more time I spend with her, the more the desire seems to grow. If only I could get it out of my system. I just need one damn night with her.

I look up when I hear a little giggle come from the doorway of my room. Tripp is standing there in a pair of small cotton shorts and a tank top. I can see her nipples pressing against the thin fabric of her shirt, and my cock instantly twitches in excitement. What I wouldn't give to suck them into my mouth and bite them.

"Come downstairs, Stud." She tilts her head in thought and grips onto the doorframe. "You've been up here for the last hour, alone. Have a little fun. Come on."

Setting down my guitar, I smile as she runs into my room and jumps onto my lap. "You have no idea how happy I am to have you here. It's all I've been able to think about for days."

Standing up, I pick her up with me and toss her over my shoulder. She slaps my ass, only causing me to want her more. "Let's have some fun then. I owe you for making you wait so long."

I keep her over my shoulder while making my way down the stairs. As soon as we enter the kitchen, Lucas cheers and holds up a shot for us to join him.

"There he is. Finally come down to play?"

I arch an eyebrow while setting Tripp down beside me. "I

guess so. This really hot chick said I have to. So . . ." I grab one of the shots and hold it up. "Let the fun begin."

An hour later, we're all pretty buzzed and talking about the most random shit in the world.

When I look over at Lucas, I find him looking at me as if he's trying to figure something out. "What?" I ask while throwing my second dart.

Lucas grins before tilting back another shot. "I was just thinking about something." He nods his head toward Tripp as she sits up from her tanning bed, oblivious to us watching her from across the room. "Have you two ever kissed?"

I pause from throwing my last dart. "Yeah." I throw it hard at the dartboard. "She was my first kiss."

Lucas is silent for a second before continuing. "Ever think about fucking her?"

"Are you fucking serious?" I turn to him, my eyes heated. "What the hell are you getting at, Lucas?"

"I want to see you two fuck," he says without hesitation. "It's just always something that I've wanted to experience with Tripp, but I want it to be with someone that she feels comfortable with. You two have been friends for a long time. There's no one she trusts more than you."

I take a long drink of my beer, my heart racing at the thought of me being inside Tripp. "Is this a damn joke?"

"Is what a joke?"

We both look beside us to see Tripp standing there in her bikini, looking so damn beautiful that it's hard to breathe. How the hell am I supposed to look at her the same after what Lucas has just asked?

Fuck me . . .

"Nothing," I mutter. "Just Lucas talking some crazy shit that will never happen."

Tripp turns her gaze to Lucas. "Alright . . . what is Alex talking about?"

Reaching out to grab her waist, Lucas pulls Tripp to him and turns her around so that she's facing me. "I think it would be really hot for me to watch Alex fuck you. I'm not just saying this because I've been drinking. I've been thinking about this since he saw me fingering you in the hall. Fuck, it got me so hot, hotter than I've ever been. We both had the best sex we've ever had after that. You and I both know it."

I can't help but to notice the look of desire in Tripp's eyes before she quickly pulls them away and pushes her way out of Lucas' arms. "Are you serious, Lucas? Who the hell just comes out and says that?" She runs her hands over her face and then starts playing with her ring. "Alex is my best friend. I can't sleep with him, especially with you watching. I know we're all game for a little fun, but that is just crossing an invisible line. That line should never be crossed."

I really don't know what to say at this point, so I just grab another beer, twist the top off, and quickly tilt it back.

"That's why you should do it with Alex. I'm the only person you have had sex with, Tripp. We only have a few weeks to figure things out before everything changes. It will be good for all of us. I get to enjoy watching another guy fuck you and you get to experience sex with someone else before settling down with me . . . And well, as far as Alex . . . he gets to sleep with you. That's all the reason he really needs."

"And if she falls for me?"

Lucas and Tripp both look at me at the same time.

I set my empty bottle down and walk over so that I'm face to face with Lucas. "I'm not ruining thirteen years of friendship just so you or I can get off. She's worth way more to me than that shit."

"That won't happen. It's a little hard to get intimate when you have someone watching you. Don't you think? All you have to remember is that it's just for fun. Nothing more. This could be the hottest experience of all of our lives. Not just mine."

Tripp grips onto the pool table, but doesn't say anything. It kills me not knowing what she's thinking.

"You two think about. That's all I'm asking. You can't tell me that I'm the only one that thinks this will be hot."

I need to get the fuck out of here. This is fucking with my head. I slam my empty beer down and wipe my mouth off with my arm. "I'm taking a swim."

I walk away, leaving Tripp and Lucas alone. I'm sure Tripp will talk some sense into him. I wish that I could, but a part of me wants it to happen, just so I can be with her once; just one damn time, and maybe I can get my want for her out of my system. If I stay, I'm going to give myself away. This is the hardest thing that I've ever had to pass up and I can only resist for so fucking long.

EIGHT

TRIPP

ALEX'S NAKED BODY ON TOP of mine as he slowly slides his dick between my thighs . . .

My hands roaming his sexy body as he swirls his tongue around my nipples . . .

Lucas watching as Alex fucks me . . .

These thoughts have been running through my head for the last hour. I've tried so hard, but I can't seem to make them stop. They're on repeat in my fucking brain, driving me to the brink of insanity.

I stop pacing my bedroom and walk over to the bathroom door to see if I can hear any movement coming from Alex's room. I haven't heard him come upstairs yet, but with Alex being so slick, he could be already sleeping and me not even know it.

I'm starting to feel panicky that Alex hasn't tried talking to me about what Lucas suggested. We talk about everything. It worries me that the idea of sleeping with me might've pushed him away. He hasn't uttered a word to me since. I hate that feeling. It's the worst feeling in the world to me. I can never lose Alex. I seriously can't imagine a world without him in it.

Making my way through the bathroom, I pause in front of his closed door before slowly turning the handle and cracking the door open. I poke my head inside and quietly say his name, even though I can already see that it's empty. My mind is too messed up right now to even think straight. I just stare at the back wall that I painted him and fight the urge to cry.

He's either still swimming or he's trying to avoid me. Either way, it's not good. Alex swims to release stress. I've noticed that since he stopped fighting a while back, but he usually never swims for this long.

I go back to my room and pace for a little while longer, letting all my emotions build up, before deciding that I can't take it anymore. I have to talk to him about this and make sure that everything is still okay with us.

I feel sick to my stomach right now.

Swallowing back my queasiness, I quickly make my way downstairs and down the hallway, stopping in front of the double doors. My heart is racing so fast at the thought of seeing Alex that I have to take a second to catch my breath.

"Why am I so damn nervous? It's only Alex." I take a slow, deep breath, before opening the doors and stepping inside. This is something that I need to do.

My heart instantly stops as my eyes set on Alex, swimming to the edge of the pool before gripping it.

So fucking beautiful . . .

Alex pulls himself out of the pool, completely naked; his muscular, tatted body glistening as his eyes set on me.

Everything seems to go in slow motion as my eyes steadily trail down his firm body, starting from his chest, pausing on his ripped abs, and then finally stopping on his dick.

I cover my mouth as a loud gasp escapes, sucking the air straight out of my lungs. I try to turn away so I can leave, but my body seems to be frozen in place as Alex stalks toward me with pure fire in his gray eyes.

Stopping in front of me, he grips the back of my head and before I can even register what is happening, he crushes his lips to mine, causing me to almost fall over.

Holding me up, his grip on my hair tightens as his kiss deepens, causing me to feel weak in his strong arms. There's so much passion and fierceness behind his kiss that it has me completely and utterly speechless. One taste of him and he's commanded my full body, heart, and soul to be his and his alone.

I moan, feeling his stud run across my open lips as he traces my mouth with his tongue, tasting me completely. Everything about his movements right now feels so powerful and possessive, leaving me damn hot and confused at the same time.

One arm encircles my waist as he turns our bodies around and starts carefully backing me up towards the water. I feel his arm jerk my body to a halt, right as my heels hang over the edge of the pool.

He moans into my mouth, before breaking the kiss and jumping into the shallow end of the water, and then reaches up, grips my waist, and pulls me into the water with him.

Our hearts beat together as our bodies meet. "Fuck, I've been wanting to do this for so long." He crushes his lips back to mine and before I know it, he has me backed up against the pool wall as he rips the top of my tank top open, bringing his eyes down to my hard nipples. Gripping my thighs, he picks me up and wraps my legs around his waist.

My eyes study his as he takes my body in, as if it's the most beautiful sight he has ever seen. His face contorts with something unreadable before he brings his eyes up to meet mine and tangles his hand in my hair.

I feel myself moan against his mouth as he presses his body between my legs, poking me with his thick erection. I want it inside me more now than ever and from the feel of it . . . so does he. "Alex," I moan. "Alex . . . "

His body suddenly stiffens, his eyes seeming to really focus for the first time since I've stepped into the same room as him. Before I can even catch my breath, he's breaking the kiss again and pulling away from me.

He looks down at my heaving chest, with his own chest quickly rising and falling, before gripping onto his hair and yelling, "FUCK!"

I'm in too much shock to speak, so I just cover my breasts and watch him as he starts to panic.

"I'm so fucking sorry. I've been drinking." He punches the pool wall before growling out and grabbing his hair again. "I shouldn't have done that."

He turns around and I feel my heart break as he just stands there, breathing heavily.

"I won't look at your body while you get out, Tripp. I should have more control over what I'm doing. Please don't think badly of me."

Pulling myself out of the water, I swallow back the pain and just stand there for a moment, watching his back.

"I could never think badly of you, Alex. I'm just as much guilty as you are." Then without another word I walk away, leaving him alone. I have no words. I'm speechless.

Holding my shirt closed, I quickly walk down the hall, avoiding Lucas' bedroom before walking up the stairs on shaky legs. Of course my thoughts go straight to Alex walking up behind me and gripping my waist for support on the way up. That's what would normally be happening right now, but instead he's hiding from me in the pool.

As soon as I walk into my room, I release my breath and slam my back against my closed door.

Shit. What the hell just happened?

I can't help but to wonder if he was sober enough to know what he did to me. I shake my head. There's no way he knew what he was doing. He was drunk. He said he was drunk.

Falling down to my butt, I sit with my back against the door for what feels like hours. I'm soaking wet with my shirt hanging open, but my body is in too much shock to move and change my clothes.

Whenever I close my eyes, pictures of Alex kissing me run through my head, leaving me breathless and exhausted. Alex was naked; completely naked, and his dick was thick and hard pressing between my legs, something that I have dreamt about for years. He was there, in between my legs. *My* legs.

All I can do now is force myself to sleep and hope that Alex doesn't act any different around me when he wakes up. Tomorrow we'll just laugh it off and pretend that it didn't happen. We have to . . .

NINE

ALEX

IT'S BEEN SIX DAYS SINCE my fuck up with Tripp and I haven't been able to look her in the eyes since. I was a fucking idiot and let my dick do the talking that night.

I had been drinking and Lucas' words gave me a total mind fuck, fueling me, and feeding my desire to have her in the one way that I know will mess everything up.

The problem is, I haven't been able to stop thinking about it since: the way her lips tasted, the way her eyes devoured me when she saw me standing there naked, and most of all . . . the way that she kissed me back as if she had wanted it for as long as I have.

I've never had anything screw with me so much before, and make me lose all sense of control. I can't seem to focus for shit and I know that I need to go and talk to her. We've said few words here and there, but nothing more. It's my fault. It's because I'm scared she may not look at me the same way. The last thing I want her to think is that she's just another girl. That's the last thing she is. She's *the* girl. Always has been.

Bringing my ass back to reality, I do twenty more push-ups before doing a set of side planks and moving on to a set of sit-ups. I've been in here working out for the last two hours and I still feel so tense that I could probably go for another two hours.

I'm sweating so hard right now that I can barely even see through the sweat that is dripping down my eyes. I don't think I've worked myself this hard for as long as I can remember. It's either work this aggression out in the gym or in someone's bed. Right now, someone else's bed is the last place I want to be.

I let myself sweat it off for another thirty minutes before exiting the rec room and stepping out into the hall. My ears instantly perk up at the moans coming from Lucas' bedroom. It's at least two in the morning. I guess Tripp couldn't sleep either.

Taking a deep breath, I blow it out dramatically before jogging up the stairs, just wanting to get as far away from the sounds of Lucas fucking Tripp as I can. The sound of his bed slamming against the wall is enough for me to explode right now.

Once I get to the top of the stairs, I instantly take notice of

Tripp's bedroom door closed. I find it to be a little odd since she's not in it, but I just shrug it off and walk into my room, stripping myself until I'm standing sweaty and completely naked.

Something about being naked just feels so good. The only thing that will feel even better right now is some hot as fuck water beating down on my body and sore muscles.

I open the door to the bathroom and stop dead in my tracks, surprised, when I see Tripp stepping out of the shower in all her naked glory.

She looks like a damn goddess, standing before me.

Her long, thick hair is dripping water down the front of her perky tits and the curve of her thighs are so firm and smooth that I immediately think about dropping to my knees and licking her body all over.

Her eyes widen in surprise as her lips open in shock. She seems frozen in place from my presence before she turns the other way and reaches for a towel, struggling to cover herself up.

She's not fast enough for me to miss a glimpse of her perfectly plump ass though.

"Shit, Alex!" She finally manages to get her towel wrapped around her body. "I didn't think you were home. I couldn't sleep so I . . ." She shakes her head. "Never mind. I'm done so you can have the shower."

After getting over the initial shock of seeing her completely naked, my brain finally registers the fact that Lucas is downstairs right now fucking someone that isn't

Tripp. Screw being naked. I'm not going to hide from her. It's nothing she hasn't seen before.

"What the fuck." I feel the rage swarm through my body as she just stands there, facing the other way. "I thought you were downstairs in Lucas' bed."

She shakes her head and lets out a small breath. "I haven't felt like being in his bed. He's free to have his fun."

I watch as she reaches for her door handle and pushes it open, escaping to her room. Following her through the bathroom, I grab a towel, wrap it around my waist, and enter her room a few steps behind her.

She looks back, confused, when she notices that I've followed her into her room. "This is how things work between us. You don't need to worry about it."

We both just stand here in silence, both of us obviously thinking of who is going to speak their mind next.

"I'm sorry, Alex." She takes a seat on the edge of her bed and swings her wet hair over her shoulder. "I don't want you to think any differently of me now that we've kissed. You're my best friend. You haven't been acting the same and it scares me."

"I don't." I lie. "You don't need to worry about that. That was just me feeling stupid for taking advantage of you. I don't want to be around you any less."

My mind is spiraling out of control, as I stand here watching her, knowing that we're both naked under these towels. It would be so easy to lose these towels right now, and for me to climb onto her bed and give her the best fucking of her life. Lucas is a fucking loser. He doesn't even deserve to have her that way.

He needs to see how a real man pleasures a woman.

"I think we should do it." I step closer to her, stopping right in front of her bed.

She looks up at me and swallows nervously as I lean forward and place my hands on the outside of her thighs. "Do what?"

Her eyes bounce back and forth between mine as she waits patiently for me to answer. I may be making a huge mistake with these next words, but I can't help but to want this more than anything I've ever wanted before.

"Have sex." I lean over her, causing her to let out a small moan as she looks up at my chest. "I think that Lucas needs to see how a real man fucks. If you're going to be exclusive to Lucas then he needs to know how to satisfy you in every possible way. You deserve that at least."

I take notice of her breathing as it picks up and the red of her cheeks as her whole body flushes from my words. "Alex, I don't . . ." She swallows hard and squeezes her eyes shut. "I don't want to lose you as a friend. I need you."

I hate that she thinks she could ever lose me. Grabbing her hip, I scoot her across the bed until I'm leaning completely over her with my body aligned with hers. "That would never happen," I say gently. "I need you just as much." I run my fingertip over her bottom lip. "I can't stand the thought of him fucking other women while you just sit around. You deserve to be pleasured just as much as he does. I promise you that there is nothing to worry about. I'll make sure of that."

Her eyes meet my lips as she whispers, "I trust you."

"Alright," I say softly. "Get some sleep. We don't need to worry about the details right now." I bend down, kiss the tip of her nose, and smile, as the tension seems to leave us both.

She smiles back and pushes my arm as I roll over beside her, wrapping my other arm around her waist. I lay here for a while until she falls asleep next to me. Then, I go and take a shower before going back to my room and just sitting on my bed, staring at the wall that she painted for me. I love her for that damn wall. I stare at it until my eyes become so heavy that I have no choice but to close them.

TEN

TRIPP

I'M ZONING IN ON THE table that I'm cleaning, when I feel something bounce off the back of my head. I swear, sometimes Harley acts like such a two year old, and I'm just really not in the mood for it.

"I'm not cleaning that up." I point out. "I've been busting my ass for the last hour. I'm ready to go."

"Yeah, so leave it for the morning cleaner. Who gives a crap about a tiny beer cap?"

I hear the click of her heels as she walks around the bar to join me by the table I'm cleaning.

"Is Lucas picking you up tonight or do you want a ride?"

I toss my towel down and turn around to lean against the table. "Lucas is on his way to get me."

We both look up when we hear Dax's office door slam closed.

"I need to get the hell out of here before I lose my shit." He looks around the empty bar. "Can you girls handle closing up while I go choke out my little brother? He's in trouble again and this can't wait."

Harley gives him two thumbs up and I nod my head, not really wanting to deal with him or ask him about his troubled brother.

"Thanks." He walks past us in a hurry. "I'll see you in the morning, Harley." He taps the doorframe before speaking again. "Enjoy your day off, Tripp. I'll see you on Friday."

I just look at him and nod my head.

"Alright," he mumbles while rushing out the door.

"Why have you been so tense lately?" Harley questions, while looking me over. "Do you need to get laid or something? I don't like it. This distance bullshit does not look good on you, sweets."

I roll my eyes and toss my towel down beside me. "No. What? I don't know." I look up at her. "It's complicated. Just never mind."

Harley jumps up and takes a seat on the table I just finished cleaning. "Oh no . . . I don't think so. Spill it."

Feeling as if I will explode if I keep it in any longer, I decide to spill the details. Well some of them at least. "Alright . . ." I take a seat in one of the chairs and Harley reaches out and tugs my hair until I'm close enough for her to play with it.

"Lucas wants to watch me have sex with another man. There . . . that's what's up."

I let out a small yelp as she yanks my head back and screams in my ear. "He actually said that?"

I pinch her thigh, letting her know to loosen her damn grip on my hair. "Yeah, but if you keep pulling my hair every time I spill the details, then you're not going to hear much. Trust me."

She lets go of my hair completely. "My bad. Sorry. I've been a little sexually frustrated since your party last week, and I refuse to call Ace and let him think that he has the upper hand." She throws her arms up to show me that I'm safe from her grip. "Okay, so what's the problem? I would love for a guy I was seeing to request that. You're not really serious right now anyways, so do it."

I run my hands over my face in frustration from the confusion that I'm still feeling over this. "It's not that simple, Harley. There's a lot on the line with this."

"How?" She wraps her legs around me and squeezes. "Tell me!"

"Dammit, woman." I squirm my way out of her ninja grip and jump to my feet. "I'm not getting close to you until you get out your damn frustration."

"I'm sorry, but you're pushing me by taking forever for the details. You know I'm not a patient woman, and mixed with an unhappy vagina I'm a bitch to deal with."

I grab for my towel again and quickly start on the last dirty table. I just want to explode. "Because it's with Alex.

That's why! Tell me that doesn't mean something."

"Oh . . . that means something alright." She hops down from the table and starts following me around the room, eager for me to keep going. "Are you going to do it? What does Alex think? Does he want to?"

I stop and think back to my conversation with Alex last night. He made it clear that he wanted us to, but for a certain reason. I'm not sure if that can be the only reason for me.

"He said we should do it. He has his reasons for it and with it being Alex and how he is, I don't blame him." I walk to the back and dump the bucket of rags into the sink, with Harley following close behind. "But what if it feels too good?" I turn around to face her and place my hands behind me, gripping onto the sink. "What if I fall in love with Alex? That's what I'm worried about. I'm just not sure if it's worth one night of pleasure with him."

Harley lifts an eyebrow and looks at me as if I'm stupid. "I'm sorry, but have you seen Alex? Have you seen those dimples or his sexy as sin body? The only reason I hold back is because you two are so close. I'm not so sure that I could say no if I had the opportunity thrown right at my face. Just saying. This might be your only chance to experience his body. Are you sure you can pass that up because you're too scared? Just shut your feelings off and think with your pussy. Men do it. Why can't we?"

Crap! She has a point, a few actually. Not to mention the fact that Alex wanting to show Lucas how to take care of me has me extremely curious of what he can do to my body. It's been all I can think about all day.

Taking a long, deep breath, I turn off the lights, one by one, while making my way back to the front so we can lock up and get out of here.

"You're right." I agree. "They do, but Alex doesn't when it comes to me. Otherwise he would have made a move a long time ago. Either that or he just doesn't want me that way. I don't know, but he did kiss me a few days ago. He was drunk though, so it probably didn't mean anything."

Turning off the last sign, Harley gives me a little shove toward the door, before she pushes it open and we both step outside. After locking the door, she turns to me right as Lucas is pulling up.

She looks at Lucas' car before looking me in the eyes. "You know that people's true feelings come out when they're drunk, right? Look at me when I get drunk. It's the only time I will admit to being vulnerable. Alex wants your body just as bad as you want his. When a sexy man and woman are best friends, they're bound to have sex at least once just for the pleasure of it. I say fuck it and do it. Do it good!"

I laugh at her and suddenly I don't feel as on edge about it all. "We'll see," I say with a smirk. "I might or might not tell you the details."

"Yeah . . . you better."

Lucas honks his horn and yells something out his window, but Harley just gives him the middle finger and smiles at him. "I guess I should let you go so you can make plans to fuck your best friend. Eeek!" She squeals. "Have fun for me, and I mean it."

"Bye, Harley," I say stiffly. "I'll call you tomorrow."

I stand and watch her get in her car, before I hop into Lucas'. I hate it when the waitresses are the last ones out at night. Dax really should make one of the men stick around, even when it isn't very busy. I'm going to have to talk to him about that before Alex does.

As soon as I shut the door behind me, Lucas reaches over and grips my thigh. "Have you thought more about it, baby? Alex has already agreed, but I knew he would. He'd be stupid not to."

I feel my heart beat out of my chest as I allow the words to come out. "I'm in." I can't believe I'm saying this.

Lucas squeezes my thigh, before reaching over and pulling me in for a kiss. "Yes, baby, that makes me happy. I promise you that this will be the most arousing thing you will ever experience. Fucking your best friend while your boyfriend watches, and knowing that it's perfectly okay. Fuck . . . me." He growls and then shifts the car into drive. "I promise that you won't regret this."

Please let that be true . . .

ELEVEN

ALEX

TRIPP SHOULD BE HOME ANY minute and I've been sitting here with a hard-on all damn day, just thinking about being inside her. I'm throwing all my fears aside for one fucking night and giving her everything that I have been secretly dying to for years.

This one night could ruin everything that we've built over the last thirteen years. I'm well aware that it could kill us, but I can't fight the urge to have her anymore . . . not with the opportunity at the tip of my fingers and the desire burning so deep that I can barely breathe. I may just be the biggest idiot for agreeing to this, but Tripp deserves every bit of what I'm about to give her.

I look up with my jaw tensed when I hear Lucas' car pull

into the garage. This is it. It's finally about to happen. I'm going to go at this as if Lucas doesn't even fucking exist, and I'm going to ease her into it as soon as she walks through that door.

If this is the only night that I'm going to get with her then she's going to get the full experience of what it would be like to be mine. Too bad for Lucas. What he has given her won't even compare after this.

Not bothering to hide my erection, I stand to my feet and walk toward the door as soon as I see Tripp push it open.

Looking down at the ground, she doesn't even notice me until my hands are cupping her face with my lips brushing against her.

Her eyes meet mine and she swallows. "Alex . . . "

"Tripp . . . "

Grabbing her thighs, I pick her up and kiss her, causing her to moan out against my lips. Her body is shaking in my arms, her heart beating so fast that it's becoming hard for her to breathe. I place my hand to her chest when I hear her struggling.

I can see Lucas from the corner of my eye, watching us, but I work my tongue with Tripp's, doing my best to block his ass out and focus on making Tripp feel completely fucking taken care of.

"Damn . . ." Lucas moans out, as I shift my hands to cup her ass and begin walking her upstairs to my bedroom, keeping my mouth locked with hers the whole way. "You're ready. Well shit . . . so am I."

I've been ready for way fucking longer than you can imagine, asshole, and you're about to get the show of your life.

Kicking my door open, I tangle both of my hands into the back of Tripp's hair and pull back until her eyes meet mine. "Are you ready, Firecracker?" I whisper.

She nods her head and tightens her grip around my neck. "Yes . . . I don't know." She sucks in a deep breath and buries her face into my neck. Her heavy breath on my neck causes my grip on her hair to tighten and for my already hard cock to somehow harden even more. "Yes, Alex. Make love to me."

Her words cause a surge of heat to shoot through my fucking body and my heart to beat erratically in my chest. I've been waiting to hear those four little words for what feels like a fucking lifetime, and they feel just as good as I imagined. Lucas definitely doesn't exist anymore.

Walking over to my bed, I gently lay her down and stand above her, looking at her as she watches me with a heated stare. I find my eyes retreating to her legs, and the way they tremble turns me on like I've never been turned on before. My cock is throbbing so hard it almost hurts and I feel like my zipper is about to burst at the seam. All that I want is to bury myself deep inside her pussy and fuck her slow and hard, until she comes all over my dick while screaming my name. Not Lucas' . . . but mine: Alex Fucking Carter.

Gripping her thighs, I pull her body down until her ass is resting at the bottom of my bed. Then I kneel down on the carpet and run my hands up the inside of her legs, before spreading them wide open. Biting my bottom lip and growling, I yank her body even closer to mine with so much desperation that Lucas must think I'm crazy, but I don't care. I have to taste her, to feel her warmth against my tongue.

Yanking my shirt over my head, I steel my jaw at Lucas and toss it down beside me. He looks like a fucking kid on Christmas morning. I hate the way that he's watching this. I hate that fucking look in his eyes, but it's about to change once I get started. He may enjoy this . . . at first.

Looking up at Tripp, I keep my eyes on hers while leaning in to press my lips against the inside of her right thigh. I feel her leg jerk as her head leans back and her hands reach out to grip the blanket. It's almost as if she can't handle me touching her there. I want to see her reaction again, so I run my lip up her thigh, getting higher and higher, until I'm just below her panty line. I kiss her inner thigh and then gently bite it, leaving a wet but shallow teeth mark behind.

This time her whole body jerks and a small moan sounds from her delicate lips. I love that sound coming from her lips, and knowing that I caused it . . . makes me love it even more.

Fuck me . . .

I lean in and kiss her panty-covered pussy, before pulling her so close that her legs are practically wrapped around my neck. Then with a growl that is sure to vibrate through her pussy, I press my mouth against her heat and suck her lips through the thin fabric.

"Shit," she moans. "Alex . . . that . . . that feels . . . crap."

She grips the blanket tighter as I pull her clit between my teeth and play with it, before breathing heavily against her wet pussy. Between my mouth and her arousal, her panties are soaking fucking wet.

I can see her chest rise and fall with every breath she takes, letting me know by the rhythm that she probably wants it just as much as I do, possibly for as long too. I can't believe that it's actually about to happen. Maybe not for the reason I expected, and a little different than I imagined, but still happening. This moment is ours.

That thought has me so wound up I tear her panties from her body. Biting my bottom lip and quickly releasing with a deep growl, I swipe my tongue out and allow it to trail up the inside of her thigh, teasing her with my mouth again. I can already see her juices dripping, and all I want to do is lick her clean, to show her what I'm willing to do to her. I'll give this woman anything and everything she ever fucking wanted or wants. I'm just not sure if she wants that outside of tonight.

Grasping her thighs in my hands, I push her legs at an outward angle toward her breasts for better access. The sight of her pussy open for me is the most beautiful thing I've ever seen, and the thought of another man seeing it surprisingly angers the fuck out of me.

I slowly trail my tongue through the wetness of her pussy, spreading it upward, and torturing her clit with the tip of my barbell. She moans long and deep, and her whole body shakes with pleasure as I lightly suck her clit into my mouth for the first time, at the same time I slip a finger into her tight cunt.

I suck and lick while moving my finger in and out in a slow, consistent motion, never losing rhythm. The way her hips are grinding against my face and her hands gripping my hair, I know that she is about to lose it, even faster than I expected. A sense of pride has me smiling against her pussy for a second.

My eyes veer to Lucas. The way that he is sitting up straight and watching with hard eyes, tells me that he's never seen Tripp react this way to the sexual pleasure he's been giving her. This is his chance to learn a thing or two. That still doesn't mean she'll do this for him . . . In fact, I hope she doesn't.

"I'm coming . . . Alex!" Her hands dig into my hair and her legs squeeze my face so tightly that I can barely breathe. I bear it, and just squeeze her thighs as I suck her clit into my mouth while her orgasm rides out, showing me from the intensity that she has definitely wanted this to happen with us for a while. She's been imagining this moment for at least the past week. That's good enough for me.

Once her body stops shaking, I reach up and grab her wrists, while looking up to meet her eyes. She looks down at me, breathing heavily, trying hard to catch her breath.

"You're so fucking beautiful." Picking her up, I lay her back down on the bed, before crawling above her and placing my palm to her cheek, allowing myself the pleasure of seeing her flushed face and chest. Without hesitation she leans into it, and kisses it gently, but then as if she just realized what she did, she turns her face away, clearly embarrassed to show me affection.

"Don't turn away from me, Tripp. Never turn away from me." I grab her chin and turn it up to look at me. Her eyes meet mine as she looks up at me in silence, her face still red. "In this moment, I want you to do anything and everything that you want. This is our moment . . . together. Understand?"

Nodding her head, she smiles small, before turning her head to look at Lucas in the corner of the room.

Running both my hands through her hair, I pull her attention back to me. "Lucas doesn't exist right now, babe. This was his idea, remember," I whisper against her lips. "It's Alex and Tripp . . . "

My words must set her off, because before I know it her arms wrap around my neck and she pulls me down so hard that our heads slam into each other's. It doesn't slow us down though. Her lips eagerly claim mine as if her life depends on it, and she bites me so damn hard that I can taste blood. Fuck me, it's hot.

I sit back on my knees, before pulling her up to hers, and then grab the bottom of her dress to work on stripping her, while keeping my lips against hers. Once her dress reaches her head, I release her lips long enough to pull it off and throw it in Lucas' direction, before claiming her as mine once again.

She tastes so damn good that I never want to stop kissing

her. This test is going to be harder than I imagined.

Pulling away from the kiss, I take a second to admire her body and let her know just how beautiful she is to me. The only thing left to remove is her bra, and watching her tits fall out in all their perfection is going to make me lose my shit. I got a glimpse of them in the pool that night and I haven't been able to erase them from my memory since.

Reaching behind her with one hand, I undo her bra, watching as it falls down the front of her arms and catches, before she wiggles her way out of it, letting me remove it completely.

She's fully naked in front of me and I swear on my life that I can't fucking breathe. Her beauty is enough to make any man fall to his knees and worship her. I'm definitely no exception.

"Pure fucking perfection." I lower back on my heels and grab her hips, only a small distance between us. I swear I could admire the curves of her body all day long. "Come here."

Her eyes glance down to my jeans, before she comes in closer and places her hands on my chest. "Are you sure about this, Alex?" Her voice comes out in a pained whisper and her eyes keep going down to my jeans as if she can't wait to get them off. "We can never take this back."

"No," I admit, "But it's too late to stop now. I won't." I stand on my knees again and grab her hands, before placing them on the waist of my jeans. "Take them off, Tripp. I *need* to be inside you."

Her hands shake a bit as she slowly undoes my jeans and then pulls the zipper down. Her reaction to me not wearing anything underneath is worthy of becoming a memory that I want to hold onto for the rest of my life. I've never seen such passion and desire in her eyes in the entire time I have known her. It's beautiful on her, and the thought of her giving that look to another man causes an ache in my chest, but I push the thought aside.

"Pull them down, Tripp. Let me show Lucas how you deserve to be fucked . . . "

Lucas moves, making himself more visible. He takes on an expression that I didn't expect to see so early on. He looks scared . . . almost regretful, as if he's starting to think this was a bad idea. Maybe he's seeing something that he doesn't like: his woman enjoying her best friend more than she enjoys him. Not only is it her best friend, but the one man that knows every fucking thing about her. He has one advantage over me, only one, and that is knowing already what it feels like to be inside of her, but not for long . . .

Doing as told, Tripp pulls my jeans down, swallowing hard as my thick erection springs free, causing Tripp's breathing to overpower every sound in this room.

I can see Lucas rubbing his hand over his hardened dick, but the look in his eyes is unmistakable as he watches to see what happens next.

Not wasting any more time, I grip the back of Tripp's neck and roughly press my lips to hers, while laying her down below me and maneuvering out of my jeans; my favorite pair.

I want nothing more than to slip inside of her bare and have her in the one way that she hasn't allowed Lucas to, but I have a feeling if I did that, then there would be no turning back. I'm not sure if I can handle being the first one to be inside of her that way. I've already been the first to almost everything else, but this would be too big. Even for me . . .

Reaching beside the bed, I open the drawer and pull out a condom. I kiss her lips one more time, trailing kisses down her neck, breasts, and stomach, before kissing my way back up to her lips.

Looking her in the eyes, I rip the condom wrapper open with my teeth. It's still completely surreal that I'm about to sink deep inside of her and feel what it's like to make love to her.

I have never felt this desperate to be inside a woman, and it's taking everything in me not to just ram myself between those sweet thighs.

I slip the condom on and roll it up my length, before I grab her hips and flip her over, causing a surprised moan to escape her lips. "Shit, Tripp. I hope you're ready." Running my hands up the roundness of her ass, I grip her cheeks, spreading them apart as I slide into the wetness of her tight, heated cunt, and push in as deep as it will allow me and stop.

"Oh shit . . ." I remain still for a second, giving her time to adjust to my size, before slowly pulling out and shoving my cock back in, even deeper this time.

She growls and grips the blanket, preparing for more. I

pull out and push back into her, rolling my hips in and out while I moan. Cupping her breasts in my hands, I pull her body up to meet mine so that her back is pressed against my chest.

This position is deep and passionate. That's exactly why I chose it. This is how a real woman should get pleasured. This is how Tripp should feel all the time.

I lean in and run my tongue up the side of her neck, before sucking in her earlobe and whispering, "This is how you should always feel, Tripp. Never fucking forget that." Grabbing her chin, I twist her face and turn it enough to allow me to run my tongue over her lips as I push back into her.

We both moan out and hold each other as tightly as we can. I continue to push in and out, slow and hard, giving her every inch of me. My arms are wrapped around her body and her arms are gripping my arms . . . tightly. So fucking tight.

"Alex," she moans, making my heart jump. "You feel so good inside me. I want you deeper. Please," she begs. "I don't care if it hurts. I want it."

Her words cause me to lose the little bit of control that I have. I thrust into her hard and fast while loudly breathing in her ear and pulling her body as close to mine as humanly possible.

The sounds of me pounding into her along with our heavy panting fills the room, and before long I feel her trembling in my arms, holding on to me for support. As soon as I feel her pussy clamp around my dick, I reach around and rub her clit, making her orgasm that much more enjoyable.

"Holy shit! Alex!" She screams out. Loud. Really fucking loud. "Alex!"

I hold on to her and press my lips against her neck as she rides her orgasm out. She's clenching me so hard that it hurts my dick. No lie. When she comes, she comes hard . . . or maybe it's just with me. I hope it's just with me. Fuck Lucas.

Wanting to look at her face when I come inside of her, I pull out and flip her over with quickness, before burying myself between her legs again.

With one hand on her thigh and the other behind her neck, I thrust into her slow and hard while trailing kisses all over her upper body. I have to admit that I'm a little surprised myself that I'm allowing myself to get so intimate during sex. I never allow this, ever, but with her I can't stop myself. Even with *him* watching, or maybe it's because he's watching that I want it . . . I can't really tell.

As soon as I feel my orgasm building, I suck Tripp's bottom lip into my mouth and bite at the same time that I release myself into the condom, deep inside of her.

Her nails dig into my back and her legs tighten around my ass, pushing me in as deep as I can go. "Fuck . . . Tripp. You feel so good."

I roll over on my back, pulling Tripp on top of me for one last kiss. I get this overwhelming but odd sensation to just hold her close while we fall asleep, but then I look beside us to see Lucas leaning against the wall, releasing himself into his fist. The moment shatters and I'm reminded of what this is: a lesson for that asshole.

Maybe I'm *that* asshole . . .

"Holy shit," Lucas says, breaking the silence. "I wasn't expecting so much passion and shit . . ." He pushes away from the wall. "But it works. It was . . . it was pretty fucking hot. I won't lie." He adjusts himself back into his pants, putting his dick away that I never even heard him take out, let alone stroking himself off as he watched, but leaves his pants undone since one hand is still in a fist.

Tripp looks at me one last time before rolling off of me and grabbing her dress to cover up. "Well you got what you wanted Lucas," she says stiffly. "Hope that you're happy."

She looks between the two of us, before turning toward the bathroom. "I'm tired. I . . . I think I'm going to bed."

Lucas looks at me and bites his bottom lip as Tripp disappears into the bathroom. "There's a lot more to you than I expected. I guess I see why the ladies keep coming around." He laughs and heads for the hallway. "I guess you wore my girl out for the night. Looks like I'll have to wait. It's a good thing I took care of it myself." He pauses and looks at me one more time. "Thanks, man. I knew you were a good sport."

I nod my head, but don't say a word as he lets himself out of my room. He may be thanking me, but I can tell he's dying on the inside. He felt exactly what I felt as soon as I entered Tripp. It was evident in both of our eyes how much we feel for each other.

Now I just hope we can get back to where we were before it's too late.

Running my hands through my hair, I sit here completely naked, breathing hard and staring at the door that Tripp—my firecracker—disappeared through.

Fuck . . . That's all I can say. Fuck . . .

TWELVE

TRIPP

SHIT! SHIT! SHIT!

Fighting to catch my breath, I fall against the bathroom door and place my hand over my heaving chest. I thought I could handle this. I thought I could close my mind off and not let my feelings get in the mix, but I was wrong. I was wrong in so many ways.

Alex . . . my best friend . . . was inside of me.

Every kiss, every talented caress of his fingertips, and the feel of him inside me will haunt me for the rest of my life. There are no words to describe the way I'm feeling right now. I feel as if I've just made love for the first time, and not just some meaningless romp beneath the sheets . . . but love. I don't think I should be feeling this right now. *Stop!* I need to push this far from my mind and remember that this will *never* happen again. I need to accept what just happened for what it truly was: a lesson for Lucas.

That's what Alex said it would be. I need to remember that, even though it felt like so much more. *So* much more.

Closing my eyes, I run both of my hands down my face, letting my dress fall to the floor beside me. Everything in me wants to turn back around and crawl into his arms, naked, and hold him until I fall asleep on his strong chest. I've never had this urge after sex. I always kick Lucas out.

If that's the case then why is this feeling so overwhelming? My stomach is in complete knots just thinking about not being able to be close to him right now. This is a foreign feeling to me after sex. The only thing I can think about after sex with Lucas is getting him out of my bed before he thinks he's welcome to sleep in it.

Alex is different. He's always been different and now that I've had him in the most intimate way I'm afraid that I'll only want more from him. I can't have that and I know it. It hurts so much just thinking about it, but we have too much riding on it. We're friends. *Best* friends.

This is all so confusing. What if Lucas knows? He watched the whole thing. "Oh my God." My breathing picks up as I think about him being there. He had to have seen the way I reacted to Alex. My whole body surrendered to his. He completely owned me, and that is something that Lucas has never been able to do.

I just hope that Lucas doesn't realize how much I truly

wish that he were Alex, or how much I wish that it could be Alex that I'm with and not him. That could mess up everything that I've had with both of them over the years.

Playing this off and pretending that I just want to be friends with Alex is going to be the hardest thing I've ever had to do, especially seeing him with other girls so freely.

How am I going to do this?

Pressing my face against the door, I run my hand through my tangled, wet mess of hair and listen to the sound of Alex pacing his room.

Things don't have to change . . . I can pretend. Right?

THE NEXT MORNING I WAKE up extremely tense and on edge. I guess if you can call it waking up. I didn't sleep much at all. I spent most of the night watching the bathroom door as if waiting for Alex to come through it. He didn't . . . and I have to admit that it had me extremely stressed out. A part of me hoped that he would and that everything would go back to feeling normal between us. It made it hard to sleep.

Every time I would close my eyes and try to force myself to sleep, images of Alex on top of me flooded my thoughts, making me sweat. The passionate look in his grayish eyes kept me fighting for air. There is absolutely no way in hell I will ever be able to forget last night, but to Alex, it may just be another night for him. He's used to sleeping with numerous girls and keeping his feelings out of the mix. I guess you could even call him a pro at it.

Still . . . I can't help but to wonder how he's feeling or what he's thinking. I want to know if there's just the slightest chance that it meant something to him. I want to know that I wasn't the only one that felt it.

"Tripp. You over there daydreaming or something?"

I snap out of my thoughts of Alex when I hear Lucas' voice behind me. He just came out of his room from getting ready for work and I've been here in the kitchen making breakfast to keep my mind off things.

I shake my head and force a smile, before looking over my shoulder at him. "No, I was just concentrating on the bacon." I lie. "I'm still trying to wake up is all."

Lucas' arms snake around my waist from behind, and within seconds I feel his lips brush against my neck. "Damn girl . . . you must still be exhausted from last night. You two definitely put on a pretty intense show. No lie. If I didn't know better I would think you two had something going on." His hands wander my body, stopping on my breasts. He moans in my ear as he cups each one, giving them a light squeeze. "I can't wait to have you in my bed tonight. Just imagine the physical pleasure you had with Alex, but with emotions mixed in. That will be us, baby. Just wait."

Pressing his erection against my ass, he bites my neck and begins grinding against me. He starts out slow, before speeding up, pushing me against the counter as if all he wants to do is lift up my dress and take me right here in the kitchen.

A feeling of uneasiness takes over and I can't help but try to squirm my way out of his hold. After last night I'm just not in the mood to be this close to Lucas. It doesn't feel right and he couldn't be more wrong about last night. The emotions were there for me with Alex far more than they've ever been with him.

"Lucas . . ." I jerk my neck away from his mouth and reach for the fork to flip the bacon. "I need to watch the food. It's going to burn."

Reaching over, Lucas turns off the burner and goes back to kissing my neck. Does he not get the hint? Is it that hard? His dick definitely is.

I stiffen even more in his arms and push him away with quickness when Alex clears his throat from the doorway.

"Am I interrupting something?" He asks with a hint of annoyance. "I'll be quick." Looking past Lucas, he walks over to me, grabs my chin, and kisses me on the cheek, his lips lingering there for a moment too long.

I can't deny that it has my heart jumping.

The room is silent as Alex walks over to the fridge and pulls out a bottle of water. I can't help but to notice the way his jaw steels when his eyes meet mine. Our eyes stay locked as he opens his water and takes a drink. The intensity reminds me of the bedroom. *Is that weird?*

Giving Lucas one last push with my hip, I adjust my dress and go back to cooking the bacon. Why does this feel so awkward? Is it time for Lucas to leave yet? "Morning. Want some breakfast?"

Alex looks at Lucas, before taking a seat at the bar and adjusting the crotch of his favorite jeans as his eyes land back on me. *Damn . . . those jeans. He put them back on this morning.* Looking me up and down, he cracks his neck. "Yeah. You know I can't turn down your cooking, babe. I'm fucking starving."

Lucas runs his tongue over his lips, before grabbing my chin and leaning in for a quick kiss to show his confidence in us. "I need to run. There's some important things to discuss at work this morning." Walking past Alex, he grabs his shoulder and squeezes, before snatching up a banana and walking toward the door. "Hey, you two behave when I'm gone." He winks and then does this little spin out the door, leaving Alex and I alone for the first time since . . . last night.

Trying to act normal, I shut off the stove and make Alex's plate like I usually do when I cook for him. I just hope that he's starving like he said, because I somehow managed to almost overflow his plate.

"Am I two people now or are you planning on eating off my plate, Firecracker?"

Alex lifts his brows and gives me a playful smile as I set his plate down in front of him. It gives me a sense of relief to see him acting like his normal playful self.

"Shut up and eat." I tease. "I'm serving you breakfast on no sleep." The last part slipped. The last thing I want him to know is that I lost sleep over him.

His face takes on a serious look as he watches me walk back over to the stove to fix my own plate. He doesn't say anything, but I can feel his eyes studying me, trying to figure me out.

Stop it!

I take my time preparing my plate, so that I can gather my composure and play it off, before facing him again.

By the time I take a seat next to him his plate is half empty and he's shoving a bite of hash browns into his mouth, chewing as if it's the best thing he's ever eaten. Then again, he always eats that way when I cook for him.

Laughing under my breath, I watch Alex as he grabs for the bottle of whipped cream and squirts it all over my French toast. "Whoa there," I say while reaching for his hand to stop him. "That's enough. Alex . . ." I finally manage to get him to stop his whipped cream attack on my toast. I love whipped cream, but damn, not so much that I want to swim in it.

"My bad," he says with a wink. "Now eat up, babe."

I playfully kick his leg while grabbing for my fork and cutting off a piece of French toast. There's so much whipped cream that it's hard to find the actual food beneath it. I take a bite and my mouth becomes filled and covered completely with whipped cream.

Laughing, I run my tongue over my lips, doing my best to get it all off.

Alex must find it amusing, because he bites his bottom lip and laughs. "You missed a spot." Without warning, he leans in and runs his tongue over my lips, before stopping on the corner of my mouth and kissing it.

As if he just realized what he did, he stiffens and pulls

away, running a hand through his dark hair. "It's gone . . . now eat up."

Finishing my breakfast is extremely hard after that. He just licked my fucking mouth and now he expects me to just eat up and pretend that it never happened. Hell . . . I can hardly breathe. How am I supposed to eat?

I shake my head and clear my throat. "What are your hours at the shop today?"

"Early," he says while chewing his food. "I gotta be there by nine to finish this girl's sleeve."

A girl . . . surprising.

"And it's . . ." My eyes land on the time lit up on the microwave. "8:45 now."

"Shit." Alex jumps up in a hurry and starts reaching for his dirty plate.

"Go," I demand, while reaching for his plate to stop him. "I'll take care of this."

"Thanks, babe." Reaching for my head, he plants a kiss on the top and rushes to the door. "Come see me later." He stops at the door and turns around to face me when I don't respond. "Okay?"

I nod my head and force a smile. "Don't I always?"

Flashing me his charming, dimpled smile, he dips out the door in a hurry and all I can think about is the lucky girl that gets to spend the next two or so hours with him.

My heart sinks as I imagine her touching him and flirting with him. That's why the girls go to him, right?

I shake my head and start cleaning up breakfast. I'm sure

that's not the *only* reason. He does happen to be one of the best artists that I know. Maybe she's not even his type. I can only hope, because there's no way in hell I will be able to deal with him bringing another girl home. Not right now at least. Not until I get him out of my system.

God only knows how long that will take . . .

THIRTEEN

ALEX

DESPITE MY MIND BEING ON Tripp the whole time, I still manage to make it through my first appointment of the day. It was definitely a bad decision to choose the night before a two hour long tattoo session to sink into my best friend's pussy.

I actually had to stop a few times and pretend like I was giving Heidi a damn break, when really it was for my benefit. I couldn't concentrate for shit, constantly picturing the little sounds that Tripp made as I filled her with my cock last night and made love to her.

I even found myself pushing down a hard-ass dick every so often, and it didn't help matters that my client, Heidi, thought it was because of her. I could tell by that confident little smirk as she watched me each and every time.

With a bite of her lip and a flip of her hair, she kept grabbing my thigh and squeezing as if she needed it to fight against the pain from the tattoo gun. Maybe it was a little, but that wasn't the only reason.

Every time her hand got higher, I found myself readjusting in my seat, making sure that my dick was outside of her reach. It's definitely a first time for that.

I've been here for five hours now and I'm standing out in the lobby, talking to Ace as he plays his video game in between his appointments.

"I saw that cute little redhead leave unhappy this morning. What was up with that? You didn't tap that ass?"

"Nah, man." I flip his hat off his head and laugh. "Just worry about your game, bro."

Sitting up straight, he looks over his shoulder at me, eyebrow raised as he eyes me up. "What the fuck? You seriously didn't jump on that shit? No wonder she looked pissed. What she needed was a good fuck."

"Why didn't you give it to her, man?" I question, honestly curious. "You could've made her whole day."

He lets out a small laugh and turns back to his game. "She was all about you, man. She shoulder checked my ass and pushed her way out the door. I wasn't about to have her rip my dick off."

"Good choice. I can't say that I haven't had a girl or two try," I admit, placing my hand over my dick. "It's not cool."

"Where's Tripp?" Ace throws his controller down beside

him. "Well damn." He turns back to me. "She's usually here bringing your pussy ass lunch. Did you deny her the dick too? You're just pissing all the women off?"

"Fuck off." I tease. "Things aren't like that with us. We're friends," I say, less confidently.

"I don't see how. She's fine as fuck . . . and those dresses." He stops to suck his bottom lip into his mouth and grab his dick. "She's just waiting to be bent over."

"I said fuck off, Ace." I growl out. "Watch your fucking mouth when it comes to her."

"Whoa, man." Ace throws his arms up and takes a step around the couch. "I was only joking. I didn't know she worked you up that much."

Clenching my jaw, I look him up and down. "Yeah . . . well now you do."

Ace is my guy and he knows it. We've been cool for the last six months or so, but I draw a fucking line. No one, and I do mean *no one,* talks that way about Tripp. I'll rip a motherfucker's heart out.

"Sorry, brotha." Ace grips my shoulder and shakes it. "We're cool, right?"

I pound my fist with his and nod my head as I start to cool down. Ace is just Ace. I know this by now, but for some reason his words really struck a nerve today. I really need some alone time for a few minutes to get my shit together.

"I'll be in my room. My next client isn't scheduled for another thirty minutes. Send her on in if you're out here still when she arrives."

"Sure, man. If not, I'll let Styles know when he gets back from lunch."

Shutting myself in my room, I start to wonder about what Ace said. It's way past lunch and usually Tripp shows up around that time when I know she's stopping in for the day.

The thought causes me to worry that maybe I messed up big time last night. Should I have gone to her room and held her? I wanted to. I wanted to so fucking bad. She's not the girl that you just fuck and let her run off, but that's exactly what I did.

I only did it because I thought it's what I was supposed to do to avoid mixing up what it was. Maybe I was wrong.

Shit . . .

"Hey, Stud."

I look up and exhale, long and hard, when I hear the sweet sound of Tripp's voice. Seeing her is exactly what I need and *don't* need at the moment.

"Hey, babe." I smile and walk over to give her a hug, before grabbing the white sack out of her hand and motioning for her to sit down. "Smells so fucking good . . . "

She laughs and watches me as I empty out the contents of the bag. "Well, I got your favorite."

I tilt my head to look back at her, our eyes locking. "I meant you, Firecracker." I run my tongue over my lips and laugh. "But the food comes in close second."

Her hands tightly squeeze the chair between her bare legs, but she pretends that my words had no effect on her. I don't need her to speak for me to know. I can read her like a fucking book.

We stay mostly quiet while we both eat, but every time I look over at her I want to tell her how much I want her right now. I want her so fucking bad, but I just chew my damn burger, hoping that it will keep my mouth occupied long enough that I don't say some stupid shit.

The fact that her chest is quickly rising and falling tells me that she has something to say too. The question is whether or not we're smart enough to keep our mouth shut.

"I want a tattoo," she blurts out. "Will you give me one?"

I set my burger down and watch as she wraps the rest of hers up. "You know I will, Firecracker. I'll give you anything you want."

She sits back in the chair and closes her eyes. "I'm ready."

"What? Right now?" I shove the rest of the food into the bag and walk over to stand above her. "What do you want?"

"Anything you give me, Alex." She opens her eyes and they lock on mine, long and hard, before she speaks again. "I trust you with my body. Even more now than before."

Fuck me . . .

I swallow hard and make a quick decision. I have a client coming in any minute now, but the urge to mark her body is too strong to pass up. "Give me a minute."

Walking out to the lobby, I look down the list of appointments and get the number that I'm searching for, before calling it and leaving a message for the client.

"Ace, if my client comes in, tell her I made a mistake

and I need to reschedule. *Don't* send her back to my room, alright?"

Ace nods. "Sure, man. I'll be out here for the next fifteen minutes or so. I got your back."

When I reenter my room, Tripp is lying shirtless with only her bra and shorts on. Is this woman trying to kill me? First she wants me to mark her sweet body and now she's laying there shirtless, waiting on me.

She is by far the sexiest, most tempting thing to *ever* be in that tattoo chair.

"I heard you tell Ace about your rescheduled appointment." She sits up, breathing heavily. "We don't have to do this today."

Walking over to her, I press my hand on her shoulder and gently lay her back down. I try my hardest not to stare too hard at her breasts, but her body is too beautiful not to look at.

"I always make time for you over anyone else. It's always been that way and it's not changing anytime soon."

A sweet smile crosses her face as she takes a deep breath and exhales. "You're too good to me, Alex. I promise you that." I can hear the nervousness in her voice, but her face is doing pretty good at hiding it. I give her credit, but like I said, she can't fool me.

"So I can give you anything that I want," I ask while getting prepared. "Are you sure about that? I'll give you a few seconds to rethink that decision," I say with a hint of a smile.

"I'm not changing my mind, Alex. I've seen *everything* that you have drawn and I would be happy with any of it."

She hasn't seen all of it. There was a picture that my mom used to paint for me as a kid. I was obsessed with it, so she used to paint it on all of my letters. It's simple, but so was she. My mother was the sweetest woman I knew, and when she got sick she would write both Memphis and I a letter every month until the day the cancer took her from us. Memphis finally got all of his letters a few months ago, when I felt he was ready for them. I didn't want to throw them at him fresh out of prison and overwhelm him. His had a special painting too.

"You want it right here?" I run a finger over the side of her ribcage, causing her to close her eyes and moan.

"No," she breathes. Grabbing my hand, she brings it under her right breast. "Right here."

Yup . . . she's definitely trying to kill me.

Taking a seat in my chair, I pull it up until I'm right where I need to be. I get ready to reach for the bottom of her bra to lift it a little, but she sits up and unclasps her bra, catching it before it exposes her breasts.

"Would it be easier without this?" She watches me, waiting for an answer. "You've already seen my breasts, so this will be no different. I want it as easy for you as possible." She lets out a small laugh. "Especially since I'm kind of barging in here."

Reaching for her bra strap, I slowly pull it down and away from her right breast. My dick instantly gets hard as my eyes set on her hard nipple. This is going to be the hardest tattoo I've ever had to do.

"Yeah," I say with a crack of my neck, working hard to cover my want to sink back between her sweet thighs. "This gives me more room to work with. Get comfortable, Firecracker. You're trusting me so . . . "

I flash my dimples at her when she smiles up at me and relaxes in her seat, then I slip on my gloves and prepare the gun and ink.

While holding my breath, I cup her breast in my hand and lift it enough to get right underneath where I place the first star. I'm trying my best to concentrate, but I can see her watching my face as I work, and it makes me extremely horny. She's studying me, concentrating on her, and it makes me want to focus on pleasing her body and making her mine . . . again.

I do my best to focus on the trail of stars, making it harder when I notice her eyes lower down to my hard dick. She doesn't know that I'm watching her, but for the spot that I'm doing, I can afford to pull my eyes away for a few seconds.

From the corner of my eye I notice her legs tremble as she tries to keep them closed. "Alex . . . "

"Yeah," I breathe. "What's up, babe?"

"Does this have any kind of an effect on you right now?" She sits up as I pull the gun away from her flesh. "Every time I feel your hand slightly squeeze my breast to move it I get a throbbing sensation between my legs, and then I start thinking about last night. Is it only me? I don't know . . . I'm stupid." She quickly reaches for her shirt and holds it up to cover her breasts as my eyes search hers.

"You don't think I want to fuck you . . . that I haven't thought about setting this tattoo gun down, locking the door, and stripping you the rest of the way out of those little shorts?" I tug on my hair in frustration. "Dammit, Tripp. I want to do things to your body right now and leave my mark on you so badly that I can't even fucking think straight. I want to bury myself deep between those thighs and ruin you for any other man."

Fuck . . . I wasn't expecting all that shit to come out of my mouth. This is bad. So fucking bad.

"I've been thinking about being inside you since you left my room last night, Tripp. I'm trying my best to keep it together for both of our sakes. Trust me on that."

"Alex . . ." Tripp scrambles to her feet, breathing heavily, almost falling into the chair. "Maybe we should continue this tattoo a different day." She swallows hard and tries her hardest to keep her eyes away from the crotch of my jeans. "Maybe we both just need a few days to cool down. Last night is too fresh for both of us."

"Come here, babe." She walks over to me without hesitation and I instantly pull her into my arms and press my lips against the top of her head. "We can finish the rest next week." I pull away and look down at her. "I never want to make you feel uncomfortable. I'm not going anywhere. The tattoo can wait."

All I managed to get done so far was four stars. Even

left alone, it doesn't look out of place and unfinished. She's right. Last night is too fresh in both of our minds and this tattoo might just push us both enough to forget everything we can lose.

"Thanks," she says sweetly. "You're too good, Alex. You don't see it most of the time, but you're going to make some lucky girl happy one day."

I let out an uncomfortable laugh. "Yeah, maybe . . . "

After cleaning her up, she gets dressed, but leaves her bra off. It's probably best if she doesn't wear one for a while, and after I finish her tattoo she will have to wait even longer. I just hope I can handle being in the same house with her.

She stops at the door before walking out. "What exactly are you putting on me anyway, Stud?"

I smirk. "Something important to me. I'll tell you about it after it's done."

She laughs and nods her head. "Alright. I trust you. If you mess me up . . . I'll just have to kick your ass. Remember that."

"Oh, I'll never forget. Trust me. I'll collect on all of my spankings later."

"Alright," she laughs. I love that laugh. "I'll see you at home in a few hours?"

I shake my head. "I won't be home until late. I have somewhere I want to stop by tonight."

"Okay, I'll cook extra dinner and leave it in the microwave just in case. Okay?"

I nod my head in appreciation. I love how she always

wants to take care of me. This woman is special, and I know that it's not an act, because she's been doing it for thirteen fucking years. "Thanks, babe."

Without another word she disappears out the door and I am left unable to concentrate for the next three hours of work.

Well damn . . .

FOURTEEN

ALEX

I FIND MYSELF PARKED IN the alley, waiting for Memphis to arrive. It's been months since we have been here together, and tonight I really need to sit back with him and enjoy a good fight, or hell, even a bad fight; just something to help me relax a bit.

It doesn't take long for Memphis' truck to pull up next to mine, parking in any random open space. It's pretty jam packed here tonight, so most of the cars are practically parked on top of each other.

Memphis jumps out of his truck, dressed in his old leather jacket, a black shirt, and dark jeans. He wears the shit out of that damn jacket. "This better be a damn good fight for you to pull me away tonight." He complains. "Lyric has the night free, yet I'm here in this dirty alley full of shirtless sweaty dudes with my annoying brother."

I shake my head and laugh at his greeting. Nothing has changed about that over the years. It's a welcoming feeling . . . strangely.

"I couldn't tell ya, dick. I don't have a clue who's fighting tonight. My ass just needed to get out and see a show." I walk over to Memphis and sling my arm over his shoulder. "What better way to enjoy that shit without my big brother? Come on, dude; live a little. You're turning into an old man."

I walk ahead of him, swerving my way through the crowd. A few random people stop Memphis, asking him if he's back to fight, but I just keep walking, looking for a good spot to watch from; somewhere up front and fucking personal. I want to see some blood tonight and get my mind off everything else that's been happening since moving in with Tripp and Lucas.

Out of nowhere some pretty brunette chick appears next to me, holding out a red cup. She smiles at me, before shoving it in my direction. "You're that Alex guy, right? You fought here a while back and kicked that dude's ass . . . I remember that night."

I smirk and reach for the cup, remembering how good that fight felt. It was one of my first times fighting with a clear head . . . off of the drugs and heavy alcohol that I had been drowning myself in after my mom passed.

"Yeah, glad you enjoyed the fight."

Smiling, she reaches for another cup from the tray she's

holding and hands it to Memphis as he joins us. "You're both badass fighters. Hope you boys enjoy the show tonight."

She waits for Memphis to grab the cup she's holding out before winking at us both and walking away to refill her tray.

"What the fuck?" Memphis takes a swig of his beer. "Since when did they get chicks to pass out drinks?"

Laughing, I shake my head and take a swig from my own glass. "I have no clue, but that chick had perfect fucking timing. I'm definitely not complaining."

Two guys enter the makeshift ring and stare each other down, ready to fuck each other up. The crowd starts going wild as the announcer introduces some guy named Cody and another name that I can't even pronounce.

The blonde guy—Cody, comes at his opponent, swinging a bare-knuckle fist into the right side of his face, almost knocking him over. The blow causes everyone to get rowdy when the guy—whose name my mind can't even remember, let alone pronounce— wipes at the blood pooling at the side of his mouth.

As he pulls his hand away and sees the blood, he starts rotating his shoulders, preparing himself for his comeback swing. After that hit, he needs something to earn his balls back.

"So what's the deal," Memphis asks, distracting me from the fight right as the other dude swings and misses. *Damn . . . that was not the comeback he needed.*

"What do you mean?" I point my cup out in front of me. "We're watching a fight here and you're worried about small talk?"

"Come on, dude," Memphis growls out, being the overprotective pain in the ass that he is. "Something is fucking with your head. I can see it all over your face. Plus you're tense as shit. You wanted me here, so talk."

I pull my eyes away from the fight and turn to face Memphis, taking a quick drink of beer before talking. "Just some shit with Tripp. Nothing that I won't be able to handle."

"What kind of shit?"

"Damn, you're quick on the questions tonight." I point out in annoyance. "Just some shit. I'm dealing with it. I wanted you here so we could just chill and have a good time, so let's do it. Drink up and enjoy the fight."

"I'm not buying it. "Memphis reaches for my cup and finishes off my drink after he tosses his cup in the trash behind him. "There. There are no drinks and the fight just ended. Apichatpong lost his ass off."

"Who the . . ." I look over Memphis' shoulder to see the taller dude sprawled out on the dirty gravel, bloodied up and breathing hard. "Son of a bitch . . . You're good at ruining shit sometimes."

Memphis shrugs as if he doesn't care. "Tell me something I don't already know. Like what's going on with Tripp. That's a big thing to deal with. You and Tripp are . . . well you and Tripp. I've never seen a friendship like the freaky one you two have."

Well so much for coming here to watch a good fight. Damn . . .

"Follow me to *Blue's*. Then we'll talk."

After fighting our way through the crowd, we both hop in our separate trucks and meet up in *Blue's* parking lot. I haven't been here since that night I left Jade's to meet Tripp here; the night that she asked me to move in with her.

I jump out of my truck. "I need a few drinks to talk about this. Until then, don't expect too much."

Memphis just nods in understanding and follows me inside. He's used to my shit by now.

We're here for a good twenty minutes, him watching me as I slam back my third shot, before he decides to jump back in and push the subject.

"You slept with her didn't you," he says without hesitation. "It's all over your face, Alex . . . and trust me, downing those shots aren't going to do shit to clear your head. It doesn't work. Trust me."

"Is it really that fucking obvious?" I push the empty shot glass away and run a hand through my hair in frustration. "It's eating at me, bro. I want more. I can't look at her without wanting to put my hands all over her now and claim her as mine."

"Why don't you," he questions. "Do it. Make her yours. You guys have been friends long enough to know if it would work out. You haven't gotten tired of each other yet, right?"

I peel the label from my beer bottle and then slam back my beer. "It's not that simple. She has a 'boyfriend' or whatever you call that douche. We all live in the same damn house."

Memphis smiles knowingly and takes a drink from his beer bottle. "We both know that's not what's holding you back. You'd win her over that fucker any day. There's not a damn thing that girl wouldn't do for you. You've been there for each other through everything. He has nothing on you. It's not even a competition."

My heart speeds up as his words set in. He's right. Lucas has nothing to do with me not making Tripp my girl. I'd steal her from him in a heartbeat without giving a shit. It's the loss that scares me; the loss that we'd *both* feel if things didn't work out and we had to move on from each other. I never want to be hurt by her and I sure as fuck would never want to hurt her. I care about her way too much.

"I know, man. I don't know. It's some shit I'll have to figure out. Until then, I'll just have to do my best to keep my hands to myself. No more sexual shit between us. Strictly friends."

Memphis snickers. "That won't last long."

"It'll have to." I finish off my beer and stand up, ready to go home and jump in the pool to cool off. "Or I'm fucked."

"You want Lyric to talk to Tripp and see how she's feeling about all this shit?"

I shake my head and toss down some cash. "Hell no. That's the last thing I want right now." I throw my arms around Lyric and squeeze her as she attempts to sneak up on me. "You're not that smooth, doll."

"Damn you, Alex!" She slaps my chest and pulls away. "Why won't you just let me scare you once? Just one time and I'll be happy, dammit."

I can't do that." I tease. "Well, I'm out of here so you guys can enjoy dinner. I have food waiting at home for me."

"Lucky dog you." Lyric teases. "Tell her to send dinner my way sometime. She's got skills in the kitchen and I've been dying for her homemade dumplings."

"Alright, man." Memphis looks up at me, before wrapping his arms around Lyric and pulling her against him. "I'm here if you need anything. I mean that shit."

"What's going on," Lyric questions, looking between the two of us. "Something I should know?"

"Not right now, doll." I wink and start walking backward to get away before she can get it out of me. "Later."

As soon as I get out to my truck, I strip out of my shirt and pull out of the parking lot. I need to hit that pool at full speed to blow off steam, and quick.

Before I blow off steam in the one place that I can't. Between Tripp's thighs . . .

FIFTEEN

TRIPP

OH MAN! OH MAN!

I don't know what made me think that this tattoo was a good idea. I have to be stupid to think that I'd be able to handle his hands on me after last night. I can't. I couldn't, and I don't know when I'll be able to again.

Ever since I left his room at the shop today, I've been imagining the feel of his strong, tattooed hand holding my breast. Every time I looked down and saw his hand there, flashes of him between my legs invaded my mind. I couldn't see anything else. I couldn't seem to shake the image off. All I wanted was to *feel* what I was I was imagining. I wanted to feel him filling me.

"Babe . . . damn, you're somewhere else tonight. Hello . .

." Lucas snaps his fingers in front of my face, saving myself from the dirty thoughts of Alex that I've been drowning in the whole night.

Even at a party I can't seem to keep my mind straight. There are over thirty people here, yet the only person I want to talk to is Alex; the one person that isn't here.

"Lucas . . ." I warn. "Don't snap your fingers in front of my face. You know how much I hate that." I push my way out of his arms to go make myself another drink. "I'm just tired. It's been a long week and I've got a lot on my mind with the bar and stuff."

Lucas pushes up behind me and wraps his arms around me, squeezing my breasts and jiggling them. Ugh . . . I fucking hate when he does that.

"Let me wake you up then, baby." He rubs his lips up the side of my neck, before biting. I slightly pull away, before he can leave a mark.

"Alex . . ."

Shit . . .

My whole body becomes heated in embarrassment from calling Lucas by the wrong name. I seriously just cannot function tonight. This is so not good. I've never been this distracted in my entire life.

"Alex, huh? Is that who's on your mind?"

Just as I think Lucas is about to pull away and get pissed at me for calling him by Alex's name, he pulls me closer to him instead and slips his hand up the front of my dress, sliding his finger through my folds.

"Close your eyes, baby. I can finger fuck you as Alex if you want." I lose my breath for a second at the mention of Alex finger fucking me. "You're so fucking wet and warm. Fuck me . . . "

Just as he's about to slide his finger inside me, I open my eyes and quickly push his hand away. He's not Alex, and this shit with him pretending that he is, is beginning to fuck with me. "What the hell is it about Alex and me together that turns you on so much? Huh? Tell me."

He grabs my arm and holds me in place as I attempt to walk past him. He's making me so damn angry and uncomfortable right now. "You act as if I'm the only one that gets turned on by it. I think we both know that's a lie."

"Let go." I yank my arm away and walk through the crowded kitchen to find a quiet place in the hallway. I really don't want his friends to hear this. Lucas follows behind me with his arm around my waist, as if I'm going to run away from him. I should, because right now . . . I want to.

Lucas pins me against the wall and gets close to my face, with his hips pressing against me. "You don't think that I've seen the way you and Alex are together? You guys sleep in the same damn bed. The two of you cuddle and shit. He even sings to you and plays the guitar to calm you down. He protects you. You protect him and look out for him. You guys are the perfect fucking couple without being an actual couple."

He stops to brush his lips over mine. "There is so much sexual tension between you and Alex that even *I* can feel it in my balls. Watching two people that have wanted to *fuck* for as long as they have known each other finally break down and do it is by far the sexiest thing a man can witness, so yes, it turns me on. It makes me so fucking hard that it hurts, and it makes me even harder to know that I get to be the one to fuck you when he can't anymore. Soon, I will be the only one between those sweet thighs of yours, and Alex will be left with a small taste that he can never sample again."

Anger floods my body and all I want to do is knee Lucas in the fucking balls. I should have known there was an ulterior motive. "Lucas, you can be such a dick." Placing my hands to his chest, I shove him backward and rush down the hall toward the back door. He can be such a little bitch sometimes when he drinks.

"Whoa! Baby!" Lucas follows at my heels, not getting the hint. "Stop, please. Come here."

I turn around, stopping him dead in his tracks. "What? Just leave me alone, Lucas! You've had too much to drink and you're acting like a straight up ass."

He reaches out and runs his hands up my arms to soothe me. "I didn't mean for it to come out as harshly as it did. I'm sorry. Okay? I'm jealous of what you guys have. I'm human. I'm really fucking jealous, and I thought that after you guys realized how awkward it would be together, that it would change, but it wasn't awkward at all."

Swallowing hard, I look up to meet his desperate eyes. I almost feel sorry for him, but not enough to lie and tell him that I want him more than I do Alex. "I don't really know what to say right now, Lucas. I'm pretty pissed and just want to go home."

"I'm leaving in the morning, Tripp. The bank wants to fly me out to New York to see how I do running one of the biggest branches that they have. I'll be gone for a week. I think when I get back that we should discuss making us exclusive. It's been long enough, and I'm ready to make you mine."

What the fuck . . .

"In a week, Lucas? One week . . . as in seven days?" I swallow hard and fight to catch my breath. I don't know if a week is long enough. I feel as if I'm suffocating at just the thought of being serious with Lucas. That's definitely not a good sign. "I don't know . . . "

"A week is plenty of time, Tripp. It's been almost a year. I really don't want to wait anymore. I can't. Those other girls have nothing compared to you. You wanted us to keep it light and fun . . . so that's what I've been doing. After next week I'm done with that shit."

I reach out for Lucas' keys as he dangles them in front of me. "Sorry for being an ass. I'll let you drive us home."

I squeeze Lucas' keys in my hand as he leaves me alone to say goodbye to his friends. Normally I would say my goodbyes too, but tonight I just can't seem to bring myself to, so instead, I jump into the driver's seat of Lucas' vehicle and wait for him. All I really want to do right now is go home and crawl into the warmth of my cozy bed. No more thinking . . .

WHEN WE GOT BACK TO the house Lucas tried talking me into sleeping in his bed, but that's the last thing I can force myself to do right now. Then he tried to talk me into just a quickie, which I declined as well. Lucas just needs to sleep his stupidity off and get ready for his early morning flight.

The sounds of Alex in the pool cause me to pause in the kitchen and listen for a minute. It's taking everything in me not to go into that room, knowing damn well that Alex is most likely swimming naked. I don't know what it is with him and naked swimming, but it's extremely hot. I hate that it's such a temptation.

Wondering if he ate the dinner I left him, I open the microwave to see that the plate of Steak and fried potatoes are gone. I smile to myself, knowing that it's one of Alex's favorite meals and that he gets extremely happy every time that I make it for him. It gives me a sense of pride.

Making my way up the stairs, I strip down to a silky camisole and my panties, before crawling into the bed and turning off the bedside lamp.

I can't help but to toss and turn, while listening for Alex to come up to his room. Just knowing that he's close by will help me fall asleep. It always has.

Not even forty minutes later, once I'm close to finally drifting off to never-never land, I feel the bed beside me dip and the mouthwatering scent of Alex fills the air as he slips in next to me, then pulls me into his cold, slightly wet arms and holds me like he's been doing since we were kids . . .

Except now . . . it feels so much different.

SIXTEEN

TRIPP

SEVEN YEARS AGO . . .

I SIT UP IN BED to the sound of someone slowly raising my bedroom window. My heart swells, knowing that it's Alex sneaking in once again. I'm starting to look forward to this very sound and I've been finding myself watching and waiting for it more often these days.

My heart speeds up with anticipation as he climbs inside and shuts the window behind him, trying to be quiet enough so that he doesn't wake Tara up.

"Alex . . ." It's dark, so I can't really make anything out except for the dark figure coming at me, dressed in a hoodie. The hood covers his face and his body appears to be shaking. He seems to be taking his time walking toward me, as if he doesn't want me to see him. "What's going on? Alex?" I start to panic as he gets closer and I can finally make out the sounds of his heavy breathing.

Placing a finger to his mouth, he shushes me and crawls into bed beside me, slipping under the blankets and getting comfortable. "Go back to sleep, Tripp. It's late."

"What time is it?" I ask while sitting up on my knees and reaching to pull his hood down. The sight of his bloodied, swollen face in the moonlight causes me to gasp and reach out to comfort him. My hands cup his face, being careful not to hurt him even more. His right eye is so fat that he can't even open it. "Oh my God, Alex! Are you okay? Please tell me that you're okay. Let me take care of you," I cry out. I can't help but to cry whenever I see him hurt like this. It kills me so damn much, knowing what his father puts him through, and what he does to him.

Alex is my best friend. He means everything to me. I feel his pain as if it were mine. "I hate him, Alex. I hate him so damn much. Why does he have to do this to you? Why? Please leave there and stay here. I can ask Tara . . . "

"I'm fine, Firecracker. I'm *going* to be fine." He gently reaches for my hands and pulls them away from his face, placing a gentle kiss to each one. "This is becoming routine for me. It gives me a reason to sneak out and sleep in your bed. You're my something for the pain," he says with a painful laugh. "Now lay down so I can hold you and fall asleep. I'm tired as hell and you have to get up early, babe."

Knowing that Alex will refuse to talk about his father and what happened tonight, I pry my eyes away from his achingly beautiful face and lay down beside him, shifting to my side. I scoot in as close to him as possible, and then squeeze his arms until my nails are digging into his skin through his hoodie. In this moment I just want to be as close to him as possible. I want him to know that someone does love him. His father may not give a shit anymore, but I sure as hell do.

I hate this so much. It's becoming more and more frequent for his father to hurt him. I'm starting to worry that if no one stops him he may end up killing him, and there's no way that I can live without Alex. He thinks that I keep the pain away, but he's wrong . . . he's always been *my* something for the pain, not the other way around.

I can hear him struggling to breathe as he rests his head above mine and pulls me in closer. It's ripping me apart from the inside out. Every single part of me hurts for him, as well as the thought of ever losing him.

Please don't take him from me . . .

ALEX

HOLDING TRIPP AS TIGHTLY AS I can, I try to get comfortable without hurting myself too much. I hate letting Tripp see me hurting, but I can't stop myself from coming here to be with her after every fight. Being with her just numbs the pain and makes me believe that things will get better.

With my mother close to dying and my brother always

out on the streets fighting, Tripp is the closest comfort that I have. My father has become a crazed lunatic that I can't even look in the face anymore. He's dead to me now; a total piece of shit that isn't strong enough to take care of his family. He's not a real man. A *real man* fights to his death to keep his family together, but *he's* doing everything he can to rip us apart. I'm only sticking around for my mother and Memphis. If it weren't for them I'd be long gone by now. Well, maybe . . .

I look down at Tripp in my arms and then I realize that isn't true. I'm stuck here. She will always keep me here. She'll always be my reason to come back. She's so fucking precious to me.

I close my eyes and sigh, before running my thumb under Tripp's eye to wipe away the tears. She's close to falling asleep now. I can tell by her breathing. I feel bad for waking her up in the first place, but I wasn't strong enough to be alone tonight. She's always my strength when I have none.

I'll spend the next two hours holding her and pretending that life is okay, and then I'll slip out of her window and sneak back into my bedroom, where everything is far from okay.

Until then . . .

"Love you, babe," I whisper once I know that she's asleep; when I know that she can't hear me.

This may be the only time I say it. If it slips again, I'll know for sure that she means more to me than just a friend, and everything will have to change.

I'm not sure I can handle that . . .

SEVENTEEN

ALEX

I AWAKE IN THE MIDDLE of the night, tangled up in the warmth of Tripp's body. The silkiness of her smooth skin against mine has me fighting with everything in me not to do something that I might regret. I didn't come in here looking to do anything but hold her and fall asleep. We've slept in the same bed plenty of times before, but never with such a small amount of clothing. Her bare ass is fucking torture up against my stiff dick, and every time she moves a little . . . it gets harder. She's always gotten me hard, but this is on an entirely different level. There's definitely no hiding this one from her.

Swallowing, I lean down and press my lips against the side of Tripp's neck while brushing her long hair away from her shoulder. I hear a small moan escape her lips as she whispers my name, her voice barely coming out.

That small breath of air is what does me in. I'm fucking fooling myself if I think I can control myself from acting on the urge to make love to her right now. She's all that I've been able to think about since I got a taste the other night, and I'm a total mess over her right now. Maybe I always have been . . .

Snaking one arm around her belly, I wrap the other one around her neck and rock my hips, grinding my erection against her perky ass. *Fuck the consequences.* Damn, it feels so good to not hold back for once.

She moans again, but louder this time, and then stretches her neck as I pull it back and run my tongue up the length of it.

"Alex . . . Touch me. Please." She breathes loudly. "I can't take you rubbing your dick against me like that and not feeling you. I can't fight it anymore. I need you inside of me."

"Fuck, babe," I whisper in her ear, totally fucking losing it. "When you put it that way . . . I have no choice but to bury myself deep inside your pussy and take care of you. Fuck! You know I'll always give you what you need. Even me," I add, in the heat of the moment. I don't really know what I meant by that last part, but at the moment I don't have time to figure it out. I just *need* to be inside her right now.

"We really shouldn't do this . . ." I say, in between each kiss down her arm, pulling the strap of her silky tank down lower with each kiss. "Just one more time," I whisper. "Just for tonight, Tripp. Just two friends having fun."

"Just for tonight," she repeats behind me, breathing out, sounding desperate. "We can both handle one more time. Right?"

I don't answer her, because well . . . I don't know the answer, but I can't worry about it at the moment.

Rolling her over on her back, I move over her, and slip my body between her legs, spreading them with my knees until my erection is pressing against her heat. I wet my lips, before roughly biting the bottom one and then lift Tripp to strip her of her shirt.

A deep growl escapes me as her beautiful breasts fall from the fabric of her shirt, just waiting to be sucked and licked by me. "So fucking beautiful . . . "

Grabbing her wrists, I hold them above her head while laying her back down and gently tugging on her right nipple with my teeth. Her body instantly reacts to it, pushing up to reach my mouth again as I pull away.

"Don't stop." Her arm wraps around my neck and she pulls me down until my face is planted between her breasts, her back arched off the bed. "I want to feel your mouth on me. It feels so good, Stud."

Hearing her use her nickname for me causes my dick to somehow harden even more. It reminds me that the woman I'm about to sink into is my best friend: Tripp Daniels. I *never* thought this would happen; yet here I am between her beautiful legs for the second time this week.

Flicking my tongue out, I run it between her breasts,

before finding her left nipple and sucking it into my mouth, teasing it with my barbell.

"Alex . . . mmm . . ." She moves her hands up to my hair and tangles her fingers in it, then pulls. I will never be able to handle her hands in my hair again after this. *Shit . . .* "Lower," she whispers, pushing down on my head. "Please . . . keep going. I need you to taste me."

Looking up at her, I run my tongue down her body, not stopping until I reach her throbbing, wet pussy. "You want my mouth here, Firecracker?" I slip my finger beneath her panties and run my finger between her slick folds. "You want me to taste you until you come again?"

Sexually frustrated, she tugs on my hair and growls at me as I slip my finger inside her tight cunt. "Yes . . . yes . . . Alex." I pump in and out of her, causing her hips to buck off the bed. "Shit . . ." She pulls my hair so hard that I have to clench my jaw through the pain, but it only fucking makes me want her more. This woman can hurt me all she wants and I'll still give her anything she asks for.

"You asked for it, babe." Smirking, I pull out my fingers and rip her panties down her legs, tossing them aside, before burying my face between her thighs and sucking her clit so hard that she screams.

I'm going to eat her pussy so damn good that my mouth on her sweet spot will be the only thing she can think about while having sex with Lucas, or any other man for that matter. When she comes it will be to thoughts of my tongue tasting her in ways that no other man is capable of coming close to. It will be because of her best friend, the man that fucking knows her better than anyone else. *Sorry fuckers . . .*

Licking her pussy from the bottom of her slit to the top, I cause her to grip the bed sheets and moan out, preparing for me to make her explode. When she has a good grip, I place my mouth around her clit and suck, before swirling my tongue around it, being sure to use every fucking inch of my tongue. I want to taste her like I want to fucking breathe.

I lick her slow and steady, before dipping lower and fucking her with my tongue. After only a few seconds I feel her thighs already starting to shake, so I pull my tongue out, run it along her pussy, and suction her clit into my mouth, flicking my tongue up and down in a steady rhythm.

"Ah . . . Mmmm . . . Fuck me. Alex! Aleeeex!" Her thighs tighten around my head, squeezing just as hard, or maybe even harder than last time. "Oh my God . . . I can't . . . I can't take it."

Her hands find my hair again and pull. I love it. I've never loved someone's hands in my hair so much before. I need to be inside Tripp right fucking now, and I don't care how desperate she knows I am for her either.

With quickness, I strip out of my boxer briefs and slide between her legs, gripping her thigh with one hand and the back of her neck with the other.

"Fuck, Tripp . . . I want to be inside of you more than I've ever wanted to be inside of another woman before. If this is the last time . . ." I stop to gently kiss her lips, biting the bottom one as I pull away and look her in the eyes. "Let's make it count," I whisper.

Her eyes widen as she realizes where I'm going with this. I'm just waiting for her to say no or freak out, but she doesn't. It looks like I'll be her first for something once again, and I hope she knows that she's my first as well . . .

"You sure, babe?"

She nods her head. "Yes, Alex. I'm more than sure. There's no one I trust more than you. I just need you right now."

Squeezing her thigh, I slowly sink into her, stopping when I'm as deep as I can go. Feeling her warm, wet pussy squeezing my dick is almost enough to make me blow; not to mention the look of pure satisfaction on her beautiful face, knowing exactly what this moment means.

I'm the first man to be inside her like this and it is driving me fucking wild. My cock is the first one to fill her bare and I hope that she never forgets this moment. I won't . . .

We both moan as I slowly pull out, wait a second, and then slam into her, taking her as deep as I can. I want her to feel every single inch of my bare dick inside of her.

"Fuck, Tripp . . ." I run my thumb over her face and smile down at her, flashing her my innocent dimples that she loves. "I'm happy as fuck to be the first man inside you like this. I'd be lying if I said otherwise."

Her hands dig into my back as I begin pumping inside of her. "And I'd be lying if I said I haven't dreamt of that person being you," she says against my neck.

Looking down at her, I tilt her chin up until her eyes

meet mine. Her words shocked me. I had no idea she even thought about us being sexual until Lucas brought it up. "Is that true, Tripp?" She tries to turn away, but I squeeze her chin, stopping her. "Is it?"

"Yes," she admits.

I ask the one question that I'm afraid is going to ruin me. "For how long? How long have you wanted me like this?"

"Alex . . ." she says softly. "I don't want to do this right now. It doesn't matter."

"It does matter, Tripp." Licking my lips, I lean in and press them against hers, before pulling away and looking her in the eyes again. "Tell me. I want to know."

Her face turns red as she watches my expression, almost as if she's afraid I'll stop. "For as long as I can remember, Alex. It's not a big deal, so don't think too much into it, okay? You're gorgeous, so it's only natural," she says trying to play it off, but I can tell it's more than just that.

Well fuck. I feel like a damn idiot for bringing all of those girls around her, and now all I want to do is make up for it. Even if she *isn't* my girl, I'll still always treat her as if she *is*.

"Hold on fucking tight, babe." Her arms wrap around my neck and squeeze as I grip the headboard with both hands and slam into her deep and hard, fucking her slow at first, before speeding up and causing the bed to slam against the wall.

With each thrust her screams get louder, until I have to cover her mouth with mine to smother the sounds. Not that I don't want to hear her scream, but the sound has me close to losing my shit and coming right now. I'm not done pleasuring her yet and my legs are definitely not ready to give out on me. That means my job isn't done.

"Alex! Deeper . . . Keep going," she begs. "You're so big . . . It feels . . . ahhh."

Her pleas cause me to fuck her so hard that I hear shit falling off the walls from inside my room. I can only imagine that Lucas is probably getting an earful right now, but I could care less. Tripp had to listen to his sorry attempt at fucking other women. Well, now he gets to hear her get fucked good and hard . . . by the one person she trusts more than him: her best friend.

The first time was a learning experience; me breaking her in and showing her what it's like to be cared for by me. This . . . this is me showing her that I can own her body and take care of it in any way that she wants or needs, and also that I can learn her likes and dislikes. I can be slow and sweet like a gentleman or I can fuck so hard and deep that she feels me inside her for weeks. In this case . . . I think she needs to feel me. I've been holding back for way too long.

"Alex! I'm . . ." I cover her mouth with mine, and grip the headboard so tight I could probably break it and rip the fucker off.

I feel her clench around me, bringing me to my own orgasm just seconds later, releasing my load inside her as deep as I can.

We're both a sweaty, panting mess; fighting for air as our bodies lay tangled against each other. Right here, naked and in Tripp's bed, is where I want to spend the rest of my night, and I'm not letting go until I have to . . . at least not until the morning. After that . . .

I have no fucking clue what we're going to do.

EIGHTEEN

TRIPP

AFTER ALEX CLEANS US BOTH off he crawls back into bed behind me, like he always has, and pulls me into his strong arms. "Wait a sec." I try to sit up, but Alex pulls me back down and kisses the top of my head, wrapping his arms around me tighter, tighter than ever before.

"You don't need any clothes, Firecracker." I can feel him smile against my hair. "I can't promise that they won't come back off in the middle of the night."

Laughing, I playfully bite his arm.

"Ooooh yeah . . . I like that, babe. Harder."

"Alex." Struggling to turn around and face him, I push his chest, but stop laughing as soon as my eyes meet his. I don't want to lose moments like this with him. It scares me.

"Do you think we can stay like this?" I ask honestly.

Cupping my face, he leans in and presses his nose against mine. His sweet breath on my lips almost pulls me in, but I stop myself before I cave. "I'll never let us change. Didn't I tell you that I'd always take care of you?"

Feeling my heart swell from his words, I nod my head and tangle my fingers into the back of his hair. I've always loved touching his thick hair. "Yeah, and you have; except for when . . . "

"But I came back, Tripp," he cuts in. "I only left because I *had* to. Fighting was the only way to earn the money I needed after my mother passed. I would never fucking leave you if I had a choice. I've been there since you were seven. Nothing could make me stop caring about you the way I do. If anything, I only care about you more now." He presses a firm kiss to the side of my head and then flips me back over, holding me in our usual sleeping position. "Go to sleep. No more thinking for tonight . . . "

Sighing, I grip his arm and get comfortable, knowing that there's no way in hell I will be able to stop thinking. "Goodnight, Alex."

I lay in silence, lost in thought and snuggled in his strong embrace for the next two hours . . . until I finally fall asleep in hopes that tomorrow won't be awkward for either of us.

Especially since Lucas will be gone for the next week and it will just be the two of us . . . I have a feeling that Alex doesn't know that yet.

I WAKE UP TO LUCAS leaning over me. My mind instantly goes to Alex, but when I look beside me the bed is empty. He must've slipped out early this morning when he heard Lucas getting ready. It's not unusual for Alex to wake up and take early morning runs.

The look on Lucas' face as he watches me yawn is different than normal. He looks almost worried and defeated in some way. "Just wanted to say bye before my flight. Didn't mean to wake you so early after your late night with Alex."

Sitting up, I blink a few times and run my hands over my face in an attempt to wake up. "Lucas . . . I—"

"We don't talk about that stuff, Tripp. There's no need to start now. I'm not worried. There's no future for you and Alex, because you guys have too much on the line if things don't work out."

My heart sinks to my stomach hearing those words out loud. I mean . . . I've known all along that this could never be more than what it is, but wow . . . hearing it out loud is like someone twisting a knife in my heart and ripping it the hell out.

"I mean . . ." Lucas sits down next to me and grabs my chin, placing a rough kiss to my mouth. "The sexual tension has been building for years between you two. This is your chance to get it all out. I don't blame Alex for getting it in as much as he can. The poor guy has wanted to fuck you for years, and now he has the opportunity. A few rough nights of you two blowing off steam and then he'll be on to the next girl while you'll be ready to move on with me. We both know Alex doesn't stick to one girl for long."

"Yeah," I manage to get out through the pain. "You're right. I'm sure he's just blowing off steam."

"I'll text you when I land." He leans in to kiss me again, but this time slowly and with tongue.

He tries to make it passionate, but it's stiff on my end. Kissing him feels so wrong after having my lips on Alex's just hours ago. This feeling is so weird. Two of my close guy friends and I'm fucking them both.

Oh man. That sounds so bad.

"Have a safe flight," I say when he breaks the kiss and stands up.

Looking me over, he nods his head and then turns to leave. Even though he's playing it off, the look on his face says that he's worried. I don't know why. It's not like he has anything to worry about anyway. He said it himself. Alex is just blowing off steam and taking advantage of the situation. He will be on to the next girl in no time.

I lay back and don't move again until I hear Alex jogging up the stairs an hour later.

Sweaty, shirtless, and out of breath, he enters my room and smiles at my sleepy state. "Morning, Firecracker."

I groan and roll back over, kicking the blankets off of me. "I don't know how you do mornings so well. What time is it anyway?"

He looks down at his imaginary watch. "Time to get your sleepy butt out of bed and have breakfast with me."

I can't help but to smile at his playfulness. It doesn't matter what time of morning or night it is, Alex always has a way of waking my ass up and making me want to do stuff with him. "Fine." I groan. "Let me shower first."

He winks. "Gotcha, babe. I'll jump in the shower downstairs and meet you by my truck in twenty."

As soon as he leaves my room, I roll over in bed and smile while running my hands over my face. I love it how we live in the same house, but he still has me meet him by his truck as if we don't. I seriously don't think Alex could be any more perfect. He's so adorable that it fucking hurts to think of how this is going to be in a week...

WHEN WE'RE DONE EATING BREAKFAST we hang out at the local diner and relax, as if we have all day to just talk. We've been coming to *Monty's* for years, although, we haven't been here in months. I love how being here with him makes me feel. It reminds me of old times when all that mattered was being together and having fun.

"So what are we doing today?" Alex asks with a raised brow.

"We? Well *I* have to go to work in a few hours. Harley is teaching me a little bit about bartending during lunch." I lean over the booth and toss my straw wrapper at him. "What about you? Don't you have like a million appointments today or something?"

He flashes me those sexy as sin dimples and reaches out to tip my chin up. "I would like to get *you* back in my chair and finish what I started."

"So you want to hurt me?" I tease. "Is that why you made me get out of bed?"

Alex's face turns serious as his eyes search mine. "I would never hurt you, Tripp." He sucks his bottom lip into his mouth and leans back in his booth with a grin. "But I would mark you forever, and that's what I want to finish doing, so are you in?" He flashes me those damn dimples again and tilts his head.

I melt. I seriously fucking melt. "You asshole . . . that's not fair. You know that always works on me."

"Of course I do, babe. And it is absolutely fucking fair." Standing up, he throws down some cash to pay the bill and walks over to my side of the table, helping me to my feet. "It's not that bad. I'm almost done. I promise."

Yeah . . . that's what I'm afraid of.

NINETEEN

ALEX

SEEING TRIPP IN MY CHAIR, waiting for me to mark her, gives me a serious fucking hard-on. She's been waiting there patiently for the last fifteen minutes, while I've been getting everything prepared and trying to get my dick in check. She seriously has no idea what those little dresses do to me.

"Ready, babe?" I look down at her and lift a brow. "Need any help getting that dress off? I can find many different ways to strip that thing off."

Sitting up with a smile, she lifts her dress up and yanks it off over her head. "I'm sure you could. What can't you do?"

I tap my finger against my cheek, thinking. "Nothing." I tease. "I'm talented as fuck." I point to the bra that she shouldn't be wearing. "Now remove that sexy as hell bra, babe. You can use your dress to cover up." I bite my bottom lip, teasing her. "Or not."

"Alex," she screeches. "You seriously have big fucking balls. Is there anything that you won't say?"

I swallow hard and clear my throat, before turning away and grabbing my gun. Fuck yes there is. Something that I want to say but can't, for one . . . a few things actually.

"Get comfortable," is the only thing I say. I tilt my head as she lies back, holding her dress over her tits with one arm. "You good?"

She sucks in a deep breath and puts on her *brave face;* the one I've seen her use numerous times in the past when she was terrified. "I'm ready . . . Wait." She sucks in another breath and smiles. "Okay . . . now."

"Are you sure? 'Cause once I start, I'm not stopping. It's not very big. Well *it* is . . . "

Her face turns red and I catch her eyes veering down to my dick, lingering once there. The look on her face says that she's taking her time to remember it inch by inch.

I lift my brows at her and she quickly pries her eyes away from my best feature and laughs. "Just get it over with. We'll be here all day if your mouth has anything to do with it."

"Fucking right . . ." I say unashamed. "You're lucky you have to work soon." I run my hand up her side, causing her to close her eyes and moan. "Relax. I'll make it quick."

Fighting to get her nerves under control, she nods her head and grips the seat. The way her chest is rising and falling reminds me of how she looks in the bedroom, and

I almost lose it right here, wanting to jump between those beautiful legs of hers. I can't do that. *Fuck.* We both agreed to one last time. It's going to kill me. I just know it.

Trying to keep her relaxed, I rub my thumb over her skin with my free hand, while working on the last three stars and then the moon. It may not be something great and creative, but it's special to me. I placed the stars and moon in the exact position that my mom did with every letter that she wrote me while growing up. It all has to be perfect, especially on Tripp. I want this tattoo to matter.

When I'm done, I place the tattoo gun down and stare at the artwork placed on her body by me. I suddenly get jealous at the thought of anyone else ever marking her. "I want to be the only one to tattoo you. Got it, Tripp? I'll always drop everything if I need to. You know that."

"Yes," she says with a hint of a smile. "Of course I know that, and you're the only one I trust to poke me with a damn tattoo gun."

Tripp doesn't open her eyes until I'm done cleaning her off and covering the tattoo with a thin layer of ointment. "All done?" She peeks one eye up at me. I nod and she finally opens the second eye. "That wasn't too bad. I was expecting it to hurt more."

Smiling, she stands up. "Can I look now?"

Peeling off my gloves, I toss them into the trash and nod at her, watching to see her reaction.

Turning around to face the mirror, Tripp leans her head to the side to get a good look. She stares at the stars and moon for a few minutes with a look of awe on her face. She almost looks as if she's going to burst into tears. "Alex... is this?"

Walking over to me, her eyes meet mine as she lifts my shirt over my head and throws it behind me. Pulling her eyes away, she lifts my arm up and looks down at the same exact tattoo that is on my right ribcage. She lightly runs her fingers across it. "Your mom's drawing?"

"Of course it is." Looking her in the eyes, I wrap both of my hands into the back of her hair and tug. "This is me showing you just how much you truly mean to me, Tripp. You've been there through everything and I love you for that . . . My mom loved you."

"Damn you," she says while wiping the tears from her face. "You just had to make me cry before work, didn't you?"

"I'm sorry," I whisper. "You like it?"

She smiles. "Don't be. This is the sweetest thing anyone has ever done for me. I loved your mom too, very much, and I don't *like* the tattoo, I *love* it. A lot."

Placing my forehead to hers, I'm just about to lean in and kiss her when my door flies open and Ace appears with a huge ass grin. "Your client is here early, but damn . . . they can wait. Maybe I should wait in here."

Placing my arms around Tripp protectively, I turn her around and cover her body with mine. The thought of him seeing her almost naked infuriates me. If his dick gets hard, I'm going to rip it the fuck off. "Get the fuck out, Ace." I run my thumb over Tripp's face to wipe her tears as she leans her head into my chest to hide her face. "Give me five fucking minutes, and knock next time."

"Not a problem, man . . . Take your time."

He's lucky he leaves when he does, because this is a special fucking moment for me. Being close to Tripp while remembering my mother squeezes my heart. I know she misses her almost as much as I do and that only makes me love her more. I swear Ace has the worst damn timing.

"Thank you, Alex." She throws her arms around my neck and pulls me to her as tightly as she can. She acts like her being half naked right now and Ace walking in has no effect on her at all. She's completely lost in this moment with me: my sweet caring angel. "I know how much this drawing means to you and it means a lot to me that you would share that with me."

"Yeah, sure." I nod my head, trying to keep my emotions under control. I'm not afraid to cry, but I can't let myself get so worked up that I won't be able to focus on the appointments I have for the day. "You're the only one I'd ever want to share it with, Tripp."

Trying to change the mood, I kiss the top of her head, slap her perfect ass, and pull away from her. "I need to get this shit cleaned up." I dig in the pocket of my favorite jeans . . . *damn the memories* . . . and pull out the keys to my truck. "Take my truck to work."

Tripp takes the keys and tilts her head as she watches me clean up. "How will you get home if I take your truck? I can just ask Harley for a ride. No biggie."

I toss my keys back at her when she tries giving them back. "*Dax's* is less than ten minutes from here. I'll walk or run . . . Take it."

She smiles down at the keys before slipping her dress back over her head and reaching for her bra. "I promise to keep this thing off now. I know what you were about to say it."

"Good. Then you know me well." I smile and look her up and down, my eyes landing back on those perfect tits in that tight little dress. It's going to be hard to keep my hands off her this week.

I know that Lucas is gone for the week, but Tripp doesn't know that I know yet. I figure she'll tell me later after she gets off work. I'm in no rush to hear what I already know.

"Alright . . . I'm out before your client gets pissed and leaves." She kisses my cheek and heads for the door, stopping to turn back at me. "See you in a few."

"I'll be there out of breath and sweaty." I wink. "Take care of my truck."

She raises her brows and holds the keys up in front of her. "I'll try not to ride it too hard . . ." She gives me a knowing smirk and rushes out the door before I can respond.

Fuuuck me . . .

She knows exactly how she's leaving me: hard, horny, and going crazy to be back between those legs. If she doesn't know, then she's fucking crazy.

TWENTY

ALEX

I'VE BEEN HERE AT *DAX'S* for the last fifteen minutes, watching Tripp work behind the bar. She's so fucking sexy mixing those drinks and she is totally fucking clueless to the fact. It makes me want to walk behind the bar, pull her into my arms, and kiss every inch of her body just to see that look she gets on her face whenever I touch her. The one where she *knows* just how beautiful she truly is.

Every few minutes or so she glances my way and smiles as I tip back my beer and wait for her to have a free moment. After about ten minutes, she finally makes her way over to me, sweaty and out of breath.

"Holy shit . . ." She reaches for a glass and fills it with ice and water. "It's never been so hot in here. The action never stops behind the bar. Now I know why Harley never wants to help me clean up at the end of the night. Wow."

I watch her in complete wonder as she quickly tilts her glass of water back and spills little drops all down her chest as she chugs it. My eyes fall from her face, watching the water as it drips further down her chest and disappears beneath the thin fabric of her silver dress.

"You know I'll take a naked swim with you later if you want. All you have to do is ask, babe."

She slams her empty water glass down next to her and scrunches her nose at me. "My dirty little Alex." She touches my nose and laughs. "I might actually consider that for once. I'm that *hot*."

Well fuck me, Tripp . . .

I push my slightly hard dick down and lift a brow at her. She rarely teases me back. I like this Tripp.

Quickly turning away, she disappears to help some douche a few stools over from me. When she walks away to grab what he wants, I see the little dick lean over the bar, checking her ass out the entire walk to the cooler. My whole body heats and I unconsciously slam my beer back, finishing the whole bottle with a clenched fist. My urge to protect her is kicking in, becoming strong . . . really fucking strong.

I don't know what the hell is up with me today, but I'm freaking out more than usual. First it was with Ace and now this douche. I really need to get a fucking grip. She's my *best friend* not my fucking *girlfriend*, yet I can't stop the jealousy as he eyes her up and down, like he wants to see what's under that little dress of hers. I want to be the only one to strip her of those little dresses she wears.

Fuck me . . .

Ignoring the dude's attempt to talk to her, she walks back over to me and leans down on the bar with a smile. "I seriously love being behind the bar. I really don't think I can handle being a waitress after this. This is amazing and I barely looked at the clock once. Plus . . . the tips are *so* much better."

"Well I'm sure Dax would be happy to give you anything you ask him for," I say, before grabbing the new beer as she sets it down in front of me, clenching my jaw at the dick that is now watching her talk to me. *Yeah, you better turn the fuck away.* "I think your waitressing days are over. You're killing it behind the bar, Firecracker."

"Tripp!" Harley rushes over and grabs Tripp by the waist, then leans her head against her arm for a second. "Holy shit-balls it's busy as hell today." She looks up at Tripp to check her out. "Are you good? You're not going to run into the back and hide in a corner like that Leslie chick did last week, are you? I can't have that shit."

"I'm good," Tripp says with a huge grin. "I'm loving it behind the bar. I'm not going anywhere." She looks up at the clock. "Or maybe I am. My shift is almost over."

Harley rolls her eyes. "Fine . . . I guess I'll deal with Mandy for the next two hours, but if she whines I'm punching her in the damn tit." She reaches for a beer and pops the top off, talking as she walks over to replace some older guy's drink. "See you guys at Ace's tonight? I better. I need my girl there.

So don't even think about standing me up. I know if Alex goes . . . you'll go. So Alex, you're going."

I arch my brows as she gives me the evil eye, trying to intimidate me. "That shit don't work on me like it may with Ace." I smirk while taking a swig of my beer. "But our asses will be there anyway."

I turn to Tripp and pull her face close to mine with a charming smile. "Want to go to a party with me tonight?" I smile bigger as she grins. "There's supposed to be this really *hot* guy there that likes to dance. He's going to need a *smoking hot* babe to dance with. Just sayin . . . "

Tripp's face turns red as she pulls her bottom lip into her sweet little mouth. *There's my sexy little firecracker.* "I suppose . . . I mean . . . I guess I have nothing better to do. Why not."

"You can't say no to me. Just admit it," I say with confidence, flashing my dimples her way.

"And that's *exactly* why I hate you sometimes, Alex Carter." She pushes my shoulder and stands up straight. "Give me ten minutes to clean up and close out. Mandy just walked through the door."

"I'll wait for you." I wink and hold up my beer. "Let the party begin. Tonight is going to be a night to remember."

———

TRIPP AND I SPENT THE last four hours playing pool, darts, and watching TV, while talking about our day to kill time before the party. This might make me sound like a pussy, but I could never get tired of listening to her talk. She's the only chick that has been able to keep my attention for longer than ten minutes, so I let her talk about her day of bartending for the first time. I love being the first person she tells things to. That's exactly why we're as close as we are.

"What do you think about this dress?"

I look up at the sound of Tripp's voice to see her body hugged tight in this little black dress that ends just below her perfectly round ass. Her sculpted legs look even longer with those sexy little stilettos that she's sporting, and I can't help but want to back her up against a wall and slip between her legs. Screw the party. We can have our own little personal one right here in the living room.

This is nothing like the dresses she usually wears, and fuck me, I can't handle her like this. I'm about to lose my mind with the next little breath she takes.

"So . . ." she asks. "Is this dress okay? I've never worn it before. It's been in my closet for ages."

"It's perfect," I whisper, trying to catch my breath. "You make that dress look *hot*. Really fucking hot."

She shakes her head and walks over, stopping a few inches in front of me. "You mean the dress makes *me* look hot. I guess I agree," she says with a cute little wink.

"I meant what I said, Tripp. I always mean what I say to you." I grab her hip and squeeze while looking her up and down. I hear a small gasp from her as I lean in and run my nose along her neck, taking in her sweet scent. "You smell so fucking good."

I pull away and release her hip. I have to before I lose it and take her right here. "I'm driving."

She hesitates for a second, as if she's trying to find air to speak. "Good . . ." She smiles as I guide her to the door. "Then everyone can give us funny looks when we pull up in the grass. I look forward to it every time."

"You love it." I tease. "After you." I hold the door open and hold her hand up, helping her down the porch steps. "I don't want you twisting an ankle or some shit in those heels. I'm not saying I wouldn't carry your ass the whole night, but it may not be as fun for you that way."

"Ha! Funny. I know how to walk in heels." She turns back and glares at me, before letting me help her into my truck. "It's not my first time wearing these ya know."

Ignoring her, I shut her door and run over to jump into the driver's seat. "I think I would've noticed if you had worn *those* kind of heels before." I start the engine and pull out of the driveway before I can stop myself and decide to stay in for the night.

"Not around you," she says. "But I've worn them a few times. Okay, so maybe just once . . . for a few minutes." I smile over at her in victory. "Whatever. You win. Just drive, Alex."

Ace's house is pretty much packed when we arrive, but Harley is quick at finding us and pulling Tripp away for dancing and a few drinks. I'm standing against the wall talking with Ace, Mason, and some guy that I just met, but I keep looking over to watch Tripp dance. I can't help it. She's the most beautiful girl here, and I've definitely taken notice, along with every other man crammed tight into this little ass room. Why we're not all outside I have no idea . . . Maybe because the girls are in here where the music is.

"Yo . . . Alex." Ace snaps his fingers in my face and then pushes my shoulder, but I just look around him, keeping my eyes on Tripp. "Over here. What the fuck, man?"

I look away from Tripp as soon as she's done doing this sexy little ass shake and set my gaze on Ace. "Yeah, that tattoo was pretty fucking dope you did earlier. I saw it, man."

Ace gives me a shocked look. "You actually heard that conversation?" He grips my shoulder and points over at Harley and Tripp dancing between a few guys that can't seem to keep their distance. "Those fucking girls, man. They're looking sexy as all hell tonight. I don't blame you, man. I don't blame you at all."

I take a quick swig of my beer and pat Ace's back while handing it to him. "I'll see your ass later." I take off walking in Tripp's direction, unable to hold back anymore. I need that woman in my arms and now. I don't care if the whole room is watching.

TRIPP

MY HEART IS RACING, MY cleavage is sweating, and my feet are beginning to hurt, but I can't make myself stop dancing. For once I am at a party enjoying myself and not even slightly wondering what it is that Lucas is doing. It feels so damn good, because I'm so used to him wandering off and not paying the slightest bit attention to me. I'm here with Alex and I can't help but to notice that he hasn't had his eyes on any other girl than me. I realize just how good that feels. Is this what being in a relationship should feel like? If so . . . I want this.

I take my eyes off Alex for a few seconds, and the next thing I know he's sliding up behind me and grabbing my hips, dancing with his face along my neck.

Leaning my neck back, I get lost in the moment, lacing my fingers through his as he moves against me. Our bodies are flush, not even a small inch between us, and I have to admit that I love it.

We have the eyes of our friends on us, but Alex doesn't seem to care. Wrapping one arm around my neck and the other just under my breasts, he pulls me closer and runs his soft lips along my neck, stopping at my ear. "Let me see you dance. I love to watch you dance," he sings in a whisper, sending chills up my spine.

We stay like this for seconds, or could even be minutes, hell I don't know. All I know is that I feel sexy and wanted in his arms, and I never want this feeling to end. This is the most intimate form anyone has seen us in, and I notice Harley watching us with wide eyes, making it hard for her to concentrate on dancing with Ace, who has now slipped his way between her and some other guy.

"I love the way your body moves, babe." Turning me around in his arms, he wraps both his hands into the back of my hair and grinds his hips against me to the slow rhythm of the music. He slowly runs his tongue over his lips, before pulling the bottom one into his mouth and biting it. "Yeah, baby. Keep moving like that. Fuck me . . . "

His words heat me, causing my hands to find his chest and slowly explore as he practically makes love to me on the dance floor with everyone watching. "Alex." I moan. "You're hard."

Grabbing my hand, he rubs it down his chest and abs, stopping on his rock hard dick. He growls when I grab it. "It is . . ." he admits. "That's what being this close to you does to me."

He leans in and presses his forehead to mine, swiping his tongue out and across my lips. Just as I think he's about to kiss me, Harley screeches next to me, making us both pull apart and flinch.

"Holy shit! You did it. You two did it and you didn't tell me." Grabbing my arm, she pulls me away from Alex. "Sorry, dude . . . but I've got details to get out of this one. Go dance with Ace or something."

"Fuck . . ." Alex runs his hand down his face and walks through the crowd, making his way over to the drinks.

I hate seeing him walk away. I wasn't ready for the moment to end. I almost feel like reaching over and ripping Harley's left nipple ring out, but I'm a little bit classier than that. "Seriously?"

SOMETHING FOR THE PAIN

"What?" She pulls me over to a quiet area and smiles so big that I think her face is about to split open. "You worked the damn bar with me all day and you couldn't even tell me. What kind of a friend are you? I'll answer that for you. A sucky one. Alex is all over you now."

"Harley . . . come on. Not right now. I'll tell you later tonight or tomorrow. I'm trying to enjoy the party."

"It was big, wasn't it? I know it was. I saw that hard-on before he walked away. His pants could hardly contain it." Harley stops to smile and wave to Olivia from across the room. "Did he give it to you hard? Did he last all night? He did . . . I just know Alex would. What about Lucas?"

"Harley!" I scream in frustration. She stops and looks at me with wide eyes. "I promise you I will tell you more later. Can we just dance and have fun? I don't want to think about it right now. Please."

She gives me a soft look and huffs. "Alright . . . I'm sorry. I didn't realize it was a touchy subject. Is everything alright?"

"It's fine." I smile, but it quickly fades, becoming replaced with a rush of jealousy when I look across the room and see Alex talking to a beautiful girl with the longest, blackest hair I've ever seen. I don't know her, but from the way she's trying to rub all over his chest, it's clear to see that she's one of his many flings. I swear my heart breaks on the spot.

I get ready to turn away, but Alex looks over and our eyes lock. Without another word to the girl, he starts heading my direction, leaving her there with her hands on her hips in anger.

187

He stops once he gets right in front of me and leans in close to my ear. "Let's get out of here. There's somewhere I think we should go tonight."

I barely get a chance to answer before Alex places his arm around my waist and guides me through the crowd of people, not bothering to say goodbye to our friends.

"Where are we going?" I ask as soon as we get outside.

He smirks and opens the door to his truck, placing his hand on my ass to give me a boost inside. "*Monty's.*"

I smile to myself as he shuts the door and walks around the truck. It's been a long time since we've been to *Monty's* at night, and I couldn't be happier that he wants to take me there.

Being there is really going to make me fall farther than I already have . . .

TWENTY-ONE

TRIPP

SIX 1/2 YEARS AGO . . .

IT HURTS . . . IT HURTS SO damn bad seeing Alex this way. The pain that he must be feeling has me fighting for breath and trying not to get sick. The last few weeks haven't been easy for him, and there's nothing more I'd wish for him than to be able to take away all of his agony.

How can someone be so strong after losing his mother to cancer, his brother to prison, and well his father . . . at his brother's hands? I hate this so much.

By the time I get to the top of *Monty's* roof Alex is already laying there, looking up at the night sky. His face is still bruised and swollen from that night a few weeks ago, and it only makes me believe more that Memphis did what he had to do. Alex could've died that night, and truthfully I don't think I could live without him.

Without a word, I rush over to where Alex is laying, position my body next to his, and look up at the same night sky that Alex has probably been staring at for hours. I would've been here sooner, but I had to wait for my aunt Tara to fall asleep. I hate that he's been here alone . . .

"Alex," I whisper. "I'm so . . ." I choke on my sobs as they begin to take over. "I'm sorry. Oh my God. I wanted to be strong for you, but I can't."

Rolling over at the same time, now facing each other, Alex wraps his arms around my head and pulls me as close to him as possible. "Shhh . . . I know, Tripp." He kisses the top of my head, and then his body starts shaking in my arms. "I'm lucky to have you. Thanks for being here."

I pull my face out of his neck to look up at him. Instinctively, I reach out and wipe his wet face off with the sleeves of my sweater. "I'll always be here for you, Alex." I cry even harder as he tries to hide his face from me. "You're my best friend, always and forever. Nothing, and I mean *nothing,* could keep me from being here for you."

He smiles through his tears and reaches out to wipe under my left eye. "I know, Firecracker, and you better fucking believe that I'll always be here for you too. I mean that. Okay?"

I nod my head before burying my face back into his neck and crying. I cry for him . . . for me, and for his brother that can't be here for him when he needs him the most. The only person he has now for family is Jack. I know that Jack will check on him as often as he can, but that just doesn't seem to be good enough for me. I want more for him. I want to be more for him.

"What are you going to do, Alex?" I ask against his neck that is now wet with both of our tears. "Are you going to live there alone? You can come stay with us. Tara won't mind. I know it."

Gripping me tighter, he pulls me into his chest and kisses my head a few times. "I'll figure it out. You don't need to worry about me, babe."

"I can't help it," I admit. *I love you.*

I want to say those words, but don't. Instead I just lay in silence, listening to the sound of him breathing until he finally falls asleep beside me. I wouldn't be surprised if it's the first time he's slept in weeks. God, that hurts me so much.

I promise to never leave Alex alone. I can't . . .

TWENTY-TWO

ALEX

JADE COULDN'T HAVE HAD WORSE timing than she did. I tried my best to avoid her, but she just wouldn't let me get away without at least trying to get me to leave with her. I noticed her when I was dancing with Tripp, but pretended that I didn't see her to avoid dealing with her so it wouldn't make Tripp feel uncomfortable. That didn't work, because as soon as I was alone she was practically glued to my dick, thinking that she'd have her way with me regardless. Then, as soon as Tripp's eyes met mine from across the room and I saw that split second of pain and doubt that crossed her face, I knew I had to get out of there and fast.

There's really no better place to take Tripp than to our special little spot. When things were shitty for both of us and we just needed to get away and be alone, *Monty's* is where we always seemed to end up. It only seems right to go there now and get her alone.

Tripp smiles and turns up the radio. "Oh my goodness. Remember this song?"

"Of course I do." My heart beats faster as I listen to the sound of *This Years Love* by David Gray playing over the speaker. Looking over at Tripp has my heart beating out of my chest like mad. My mind hasn't changed about this song and how it makes me feel. It's fucking beautiful. "And I still meant what I said about singing this to the girl I fall in love with. When I fall in love, she will know for sure."

Tripp quickly looks away and pretends to be looking at something out the window. She clears her throat a few times before speaking. "I think I can already see the roof of *Monty's*. I didn't realize you could see it from a few blocks over."

I laugh to myself and just go with it, wanting to change the mood as much as she does. "Yeah, neither did I."

After pulling up behind *Monty's* I help Tripp out of my truck and grip the ladder to the roof right behind her. The whole way up all I can think about is lifting up that little dress and slowly teasing her pussy with my tongue all the way to the top. I'd be sure to catch her when she falls. That's the one thing I can promise.

"Wow." Tripp smiles so sweetly when we reach the top that I know she has to be thinking about all the memories we've made here. "I've almost forgotten just how beautiful it is up here at night."

Walking over to our spot, I lay down and pull her down beside me. "I haven't," I say with certainty. "I don't think I could ever forget." When I look over at her, she's smiling up at the sky. She's so painfully beautiful that it hurts. "Come here." I pull her onto my chest and wrap my arms around her head. "I don't know why I let us go as long as we have without coming here."

"Same here." She places her hand over my chest and buries her face into my neck like old times. The action is all too familiar, but the feeling of it is totally different than it's ever been before.

"Tripp . . ." I tangle my hands in her soft hair as she fights to look up at me. "You're fucking beautiful. So damn beautiful."

She gets ready to speak, but I cut her off by pressing my lips to hers. My heart skips a beat and a need so overwhelming takes over as soon as her lips melt into mine and that's when I know for sure that I'm falling.

"Alex," she whispers as soon as our lips finally part. "We said we—."

"I know." I flip her over and lay myself between her legs. "Let's forget about that right now." I run my thumb under her eye and capture her gaze, holding it. "Okay?"

She nods her head. "Okay," she breathes.

Within seconds both of us are naked and a tangled mess, as we find each other's mouth's again. I slide my hand under her neck and gently guide myself between her legs. I slowly push into her, moaning as her sweet tightness hugs me completely.

We both hold each other, as if we can't breathe without the other as I slowly pump in and out of her, wanting to feel every inch of her body that I can.

Every move between us is filled with a passion that I've only dreamt of ever having with a woman; with *this* woman, but I thought it was impossible. I'm absolutely desperate to be inside her right now and I don't care if she fucking knows.

Her body moves with mine, her nails digging into my back as I slowly grind my hips, being sure to hit every spot of pleasure I can find. Hearing her moan and feeling her grip on me tighten pushes me over the edge, making me want to pleasure her even more. Tripp deserves the most intense pleasure that is even possible.

Being inside her this way feels too good emotionally and physically, and I can't help but to feel selfish and only want it to be me from now on. The thought of Lucas coming back in six days has me pushing myself so deep that I cause her to cry out in pain. "Shit . . ." I place my forehead to hers for a second so I can collect myself. "Sorry."

"It's okay," she whispers. "Please don't stop."

Bringing her legs over my shoulders, I slightly lift her hips and rock into her, biting the side of her calf as I bury myself inside and stop. "I love being inside you, babe. Fuck, you feel so good."

Both of our bodies are covered in sweat. We're both breathless and completely lost in each other as I continue to pump deep and slow for what feels like hours, but I don't care because I can't get enough of her right now.

Wanting to be even closer to her, I sit on my knees and bring her body up to straddle my lap. Our bodies are plastered together, not even an inch of breathing room as I kiss her flesh all over and bury myself inside her, pretending that she's completely mine and I'm completely hers. In this moment . . . we are.

I feel her nails dig into my skin and her breathing picks up next to my ear. "I want to come with you, Alex. I'm so damn close. I don't know if I can hold back anymore."

Holding her as tightly as possible, I press my lips to hers and sway my hips, pulling her body so I can get as deep as I can without hurting her again. I feel myself close to orgasm, so I suck her bottom lip into my mouth, moaning as she clenches around my cock.

A few slow seconds later, I rock into her one last time, releasing my load inside her, being sure that she gets every last drop. Fuck . . . what that does to me, knowing that Lucas has never been inside her like this. Her pussy is filled with only my cum, and that does something to me that I don't understand.

"Shit . . . Alex," she says breathless. "I've never felt this good in my entire life. I have no idea how you do it, but you seem to know all the right things to take care of me."

She lifts off of me and falls down next to me, lying flat on her back while fighting to catch her breath.

Feeling completely lost in some other world, I clean her

off with my shirt and lay next to her, pulling her close to me. "I know you better than anyone else. Never forget that . . . "

She doesn't say anything more, so neither do I. Instead, we both just lay here in silence, staring up at the night sky. Nothing else really needs to be said . . . tonight.

This moment is perfect and I'm going to keep it that way for as long as I can.

Until the morning comes and I have to go back to pretending . . .

TWENTY-THREE

TRIPP

IT'S BEEN A COUPLE DAYS since our night on the rooftop, but I can't seem to get it out of my mind. I'm dying to be close to Alex and spend time with him, but between his endless appointments and Dax asking me to take on extra hours at the bar, we haven't had much time together.

Well, besides sleeping. He's fallen asleep in my bed every night, but hasn't made a move to touch me sexually and it's been driving me insane, leaving me with a need that I've never experienced before.

Lucas will be back in four days; four short days and I can't help but to want as much alone time with Alex as I can get. I may be selfish, but I can't seem to care right now. Alex is all that I've been able to think about.

He should be home from work any minute now. At least I'm hoping, so that we can hang out and finally do something besides *sleep* together.

I jump when Alex pokes his head into my room and slaps the doorframe, surprising me. "Change into some shorts and an old shirt. We're going riding tonight. It's going to get dirty." He lifts his eyebrows. "Very dirty."

"Oh yeah . . . what's your version of *very dirty*?"

He bites his bottom lip and growls, as he looks me up and down. "Dirty enough for me to give you a shower later. Now get dressed. Fast."

My heart skips a beat when he yanks his shirt off while disappearing down the hall toward his room. He's going back to my dirty Alex and I'll admit that I *love* this side of him.

It's been a few years since he's taken me mud riding and I miss it. I could definitely use the rush right now, not to mention . . . getting dirty with Alex is every girl's dream.

I do what Alex said and quickly change into some shorts and an old shirt, before walking through the bathroom and opening Alex's door. "I'm ready, stud. You have a lot of riding to make up. I want it fast and dirty. No holding back."

Alex grins while pulling up his old pair of holy jeans. Fuck me. I haven't seen those in a while. They were always his riding jeans and he looks sexy as sin in them. "Easy, firecracker." He winks and throws on an old black V-neck. "I never hold back. Fast and dirty is what I'm known for."

Oh fuck me . . . that mouth. I want it all over me.

I pull the hair tie off my wrist and throw my hair into a messy bun, ready to get *dirty*. "All windows down?"

He laughs and kisses me on the side of the head, before guiding me through his room. "You know it . . ."

It takes about twenty minutes to get to our special riding spot. It's muddy as hell and full of bumps and hills, making it the perfect spot. The thrill is one of the best feelings in the world, and doing it with Alex has always made it that much better.

He turns to me and flashes his sexy as sin dimples. "Hold on tight, baby. I haven't taken this old truck out in a long time. I'm ready to play hard . . ."

My heart starts beating fast from adrenaline as Alex punches the gas and we start flying through the mud, slipping and sliding with no other cares in the world; just like when we were young, stupid, and trying to find a way to escape.

"Whoa!" I scream while gripping onto anything I can grab. Mud splashes through the windows, sticking to my face. Alex looks over at me, muddy, my mouth gaping open and laughs at me, then turns the wheel and slams on the gas and brake at the same time.

"Hell yeah!" Reaching over, Alex pulls me into his lap and wraps his arms around my waist. "Ride it, baby."

Smiling, I grip the wheel and push Alex's legs out of the way, ready to tear through this mud and dirty us both. Alex has always loved being in charge when it comes to riding, but I have a feeling it turns him on to see a girl driving his truck. I'm not saying no to that.

I slam on the gas, gliding through the mud between trees, feeling Alex getting hard beneath me.

Focus Tripp. Do not think about his . . . Ooh . . . his boner. I feel Alex grind his hips beneath me, pulling me even further into his muscular lap as he releases a small growl next to my ear. I would definitely rather do *that* kind of riding over *this* kind any day.

Alex's hands stay wrapped around me for the next forty minutes or so as I do everything in my power to get him as muddy as possible. Unfortunately, getting him muddy meant me eating mud a few times, but it was so worth it.

Dirty Alex is the best Alex. *Did I already mention that?*

"Damn girl." Alex lifts me up, setting me back over into the passenger seat once coming to a stop and shifting the truck into park. "I've never seen you ride so hard." He pulls his bottom lip into his mouth and bites it, before grinning. "Tastes like mud. Fucking delicious."

We both laugh, me a little harder than him, but I can't help it. The faces he makes can keep me entertained for hours. His animated eyebrows say it all.

"You like the taste of mud, huh? Does it taste good?" I tease. Wiping mud off the side of my face I fling it at Alex's face.

He lifts a brow as it splatters across his lips. "You want to find out?" Reaching over, he grabs the back of my head and pulls me in for a deep, hard kiss, being sure to smear the mud across my lips.

"Hey!" I run my arm across my mouth, wiping the mud

off while playfully punching him in the arm as he laughs at me. "Alright, that just made it worse. Gross." I spit, trying to get the mud out of my mouth.

Grinning, Alex pulls his shirt off and turns it inside out. "Here . . ." He reaches over and starts cleaning my mouth off. "Let me help you with that."

My heart starts racing and a warm sensation floods through me as I study his eyes, carefully watching my lips with concentration. His eyes are so soft and caring as he cleans me off. He appears to be using this moment to show me how he can take care of me. "Thanks," I whisper when he pulls away.

"I got you, baby. No worries." He leans over me and reaches into the glove compartment, pulling out a brown paper bag. "I made dinner this time. Let's go eat." He hops out of the truck and I follow his lead, meeting him at the back of his truck.

Pulling the tailgate down, he opens the black trunk in the back of his truck and pulls out a blanket, spreading it out. Then he grabs me by the hips and lifts me up, setting me on the edge of the tailgate. "Mmm . . . a nice little dinner in the mud." I look down at my muddy hands and laugh. "Maybe we should've brought some water."

Alex hops up beside me and reaches into the trunk again, pulling out three waters. "Gotcha covered. Hold your hands out."

I smile and hold my hands out as Alex unscrews the cap of the bottled water and begins washing my hands off with it. "Very nice," I say impressed. "Much better than last time."

He quickly rinses his hands off and shrugs his shoulders. "What can I say? I learn from my mistakes." He smiles over at me. "And I listen. I always listen to you. I'll admit that I like to impress you."

"Okay," I say, while unwrapping my turkey wrap. "Well you definitely do a good job with that, Alex Carter."

We both smile in satisfaction and spend the next twenty minutes eating. For thirty minutes or so following dinner, we lie down, just staring up at the stars.

It's so peaceful being out here with him. It's just another one of *our places* that I've always loved going to together. This man holds so many special memories in my life that he almost feels like my *whole* life. I can never imagine him not being here for me.

"You ready?" He asks, pulling me away from my stargazing.

I peel some dried mud off the side of his face and lift a brow. "Yeah . . . although this mud is really looking good on you."

He jumps to the ground and grabs my hips to help me down. "I'll look even better with you cleaning it off my body." Clearing his throat, he walks away as if what he just said was a mistake. "We should get going."

We're both silent on the ride home, me looking over at him every few minutes, doing my best to read his face. He's got that damn poker face in place again, and it's driving me mad. Maybe it's best if I just go straight to my room and lock myself in for the night, before we both end up doing something stupid again. Maybe this being friends *without benefits* isn't going to work so easily.

Once we get back to the house, Alex heads toward the downstairs shower. "Go get cleaned up and then I'll play for you. I'm going to shower down here."

I swallow. "Yeah . . . I would love that." My eyes trail down the back of his fit body, stopping on his perfect ass in those dirty, ripped up jeans. "I'll just shower upstairs."

Jogging up the stairs, I shut my door behind me and let out a long, hard breath. My body is going crazy with need, knowing that he's about to strip. I want to be the one to clean the mud off his sexy body. I want to be the one to watch as the water pours down him. I want to touch his body so badly that I can't even think straight.

The shower downstairs turns on, making me open my eyes and remember what I should be doing. "Dammit, Tripp. Wake the fuck up and get over Alex."

Stripping and throwing my dirty clothes into a pile beside my bed, I close myself into the bathroom and start my own shower.

Stepping inside, I close my eyes, letting the steaming hot water run down my dirty body. It feels so good just letting the hot temperature wash over me.

Not expecting it, I jump and let out a small scream when I feel Alex step in behind me and brush my hair over my shoulder.

"Sorry," he whispers next to my ear. "I got you dirty . . . I want to be the one to clean you off." He runs his tongue up the side of my neck and growls. "Just relax and let me do all the work."

Breathing heavily, I lean into Alex's chest as he reaches around to clean the front of my body. Instead of using my loofah he puts the soap straight into his strong, sexy, tattooed hands and begins rubbing me down, starting on my chest.

I suck in a breath and try my best not to shake when his hands slowly move downward to start working on my breasts. "Alex . . ." I let out a moan and place my hand behind me, gripping his muscular thigh. "Ooohhh . . . that feels so good." My grip on his thigh tightens as he growls into my ear and moves his hands lower.

His hands move slowly and torturously, until I finally feel two of his fingers spread me apart and start massaging my already swollen clit.

"You're so fucking dirty, Tripp," he whispers breathlessly into my ear. "I'm not stopping until you're clean . . . "

I can't talk. Hell . . . I can't even breathe. His fingers are so damn talented. I've never seen anyone work them the way he does. My whole body is about to break down and go into convulsion.

"Aren't you going to clean me, firecracker?" He continues to rub my clit with one finger, while slipping another inside of me. "You got me so fucking dirty."

I let out a gasp as I feel him press his thick, hard dick against my ass while shoving his finger in so damn deep that I almost come undone from his fingers.

"Yes," I say in a whisper.

"Touch me." With his free hand he reaches for my hand and wraps it around his throbbing dick. "Fuck me . . . Wrap those fingers around me and own me." I start running my hand up and down his slick dick, my heart beating so fast that I can hardly breathe. His erection is so thick that I can't even get my hand around him. "Yes," he growls.

The faster he pumps into me, the faster I stroke him in my hand.

When he wraps one arm around my neck and bites into my shoulder I lose it.

"Oh yes . . . yes . . . oooohhh . . . fuck!" As soon as Alex feels me clamping around his finger, he shoves another one inside and holds me up, while I shake in his protective arms.

"Yes, baby. Come undone for me," he whispers against my neck. "Keep going. I want it all."

He waits until I'm completely done, before slowly pulling his fingers out and sucking them into his mouth. "So fucking good, but I'm not done cleaning you yet."

Pushing my back down, he drops down to his knees behind me, grips my thighs hard . . . and runs the tip of his tongue down my ass crack, stopping on my pussy.

My whole body shakes, which causes Alex to growl against my pussy. "Fuck me . . . fuck . . ." he says harshly. "Hold onto the fucking wall. Don't let go."

His tongue is like magic against my already throbbing pussy. Within seconds I am coming again, but with Alex's tongue inside me instead.

"Shit . . ." Turning me around, Alex grabs both of my hands and wraps them around his dick. "Yes . . . fuck!"

With just a few strokes, Alex's hot cum hits my stomach, covering me all the way up to my breasts. The feel of Alex coating me with *his* orgasm, that I caused, has me closing my eyes and fighting for breath.

This is the hottest thing in the world to me. I want to feel him everywhere, even though I can't admit it aloud. Alex Carter: my best friend and the world's champion in giving orgasms. I think I might just faint right now.

Breathing heavily, Alex places his forehead to mine and wraps his hands into the back of my hair. "Sorry," he whispers. "I couldn't help myself. Not tonight."

"That's okay," I say honestly. "I wanted to touch you too. I'm trying not to. I'm really trying."

"Me too, babe. It's so fucking hard." Opening the curtain, Alex grabs for the nearest towel. "I'll let you finish showering." He looks me up and down with pained eyes. It almost looks as if he's hurting. "I won't touch you again, Tripp. I'll grab my guitar and meet you in bed."

As soon as the curtain closes and I hear Alex disappear into his room, I lose it. I fall against the wall and place both of my hands over my chest. This is getting too hard. My need to be with him is too much. It scares me.

Hearing him say, *I won't touch you again, Tripp,* felt like a knife twisting in my chest. It hurt. Why did it hurt so damn bad?

I've completely fallen in love with my best friend, and

just the thought of this ending and him going back to being with other girls feels as if my world is ending. I'm completely fucked . . .

TWENTY-FOUR

ALEX

I WAKE EARLY IN THE morning, wrapped in Tripp's half naked body. I wasn't going to sleep in her bed last night, but after playing my guitar for a while and seeing the look in her eyes when I was about to leave, I caved. That look killed me. Sleeping in her bed has always been something that I've done growing up, so why not allow myself to still do it? After Lucas comes back, I may not get the opportunity again.

Fuuuck me . . . That thought pisses me the hell off.

I'm completely lost in this woman and there's not a damn thing I can do about it but force myself to treat her like I used to; like my best friend, and not someone that I want to make love to until the early hours of the morning. I never knew that falling for your best friend could hurt so fucking much, but I wouldn't change this feeling for the world. She's always been the one thing to keep my pain away, and now because of me she will be the cause of it.

From the rhythm of her heavy breathing I know that she's still deeply asleep, so I lean over and allow myself to kiss the corner of her mouth one last time. My chest fucking aches as I pull away and watch her twitch a little from my touch.

I need some fresh air. I feel as if I'm suffocating in here, wanting to do the things that I know I need to put an end to. If I stay here with Tripp I know I'm going to ruin us both. I can't allow that.

Jumping out of bed, but being careful not to wake her, I throw on my shirt and head outside for a run; a long fucking run, and I'm hoping it will do something to ease this tightness in my chest. I need some kind of release, anything at this point, and the way I've been feeling lately . . . fighting off steam sounds good. I need to stay away from that lifestyle and I know it. Memphis will kill my ass if I end up back in the alley. Looks like I'll be spending a lot of time getting acquainted with these open roads.

In the whole hour or more that I've been running, Tripp hasn't left my mind yet. That worries me. The more I think about Lucas coming home and me not being able to touch her like I have for the last week, the stronger my anger grows, and a resentment towards Lucas builds. Running isn't doing shit to put the flame out that is burning in my chest.

That asshole will be the one touching her, tasting her,

and sleeping next to her at night. Not me. Not fucking me.

"Fucking shit!"

Stopping, I grip my sweaty hair and stand here for a moment, hating myself. I let this happen. I'm the one that kissed Tripp in the first place and talked her into thinking that everything would be okay. I'm the one that wanted to make love to her in front of Lucas to show him how she should be treated. It's my fault that things may never be the same between us. I was weak. She makes me weak, even though I've fought hard to be nothing but strong for her over the years.

Leaning over I grip my knees and fight to catch my breath. I need to do something. The question is . . . What the fuck am I supposed to do? I've fallen so deep that I may not have any other choice but to pull her under with me.

I start running again, fast and hard. I run for what feels like forever; my body aching, my lungs about to explode, and my heart fucking hurting for Tripp.

Two hours later I'm standing outside the back of our house, letting myself in through the gate. I'm surprised when I see Tripp sitting next to the pool in her panties and a tank top. I instantly get hard, and hate myself for not being able to fight it.

"Hi," she says as I close the gate behind me. "You look exhausted."

"I should still be out there, honestly." Yanking my shirt off, I run it over my face and head, wiping away the sweat that is pouring down my body. I see her eyes taking in my flexing muscles, working their way down to my erection, and it does nothing to rid my dirty thoughts of her. "You're awake," I say, in hopes to keep my dirty mouth in check. "It's early."

She inhales and starts splashing her feet in the water. I hate seeing her look stressed, and I hate it even more that I might be the cause of it. "Yeah, Lucas sent me a text and woke me up. I noticed that you were gone and couldn't go back to sleep. I needed some fresh air."

I hate knowing that she was talking to Lucas this morning, and a part of me wants to know if she misses him. I probably shouldn't ask, but . . .

"Do you miss him, Tripp?"

Her face looks pained when her eyes meet mine, but she quickly shakes it off and goes back to splashing her legs in the water, going deeper this time. It's as if she wants to avoid my question. "I don't know . . . "

I swallow hard and take a seat beside her, dipping my legs into the water and wrapping them around hers, capturing them. "I don't think you do," I say honestly. I pull her closer to me and push her hair behind her shoulder, letting my eyes take in her beauty. All I can think about is biting that sexy neck and then soothing it with my tongue. *Control Alex. Fucking control.* "I think we both know that you two don't belong together. I think you're just settling and I fucking hate it. He's an idiot and you can do way better." *So much for control . . .*

"Alex . . ." She pulls her legs out of mine and jumps to her feet. I hate the look on her face as she looks down at me.

She's questioning me with her eyes, pleading with me not to go there. It's a look I don't see often from her. "I really don't want to talk about this again. You guys used to be really close. I don't get what changed that."

"You," I admit. "My protectiveness over you won over all the other bullshit of being his friend. You've been my top priority since day one, and your happiness is at the top of my every day fucking list, dammit."

I stand up and pull her in for a hug, showing her I'm fucking sorry and I'm an idiot, when her eyes begin to glisten. "The last thing I ever want to do is make you cry, babe." I press my lips to the top of her head and rock her back and forth in my arms, comforting her. "I'm sorry. I'm here for you no matter what. Never forget that. That's all I'm trying to say. I'm trying to look out for you. I *need* to look out for you. It's how I survive."

"I know . . . I don't . . ." She stops talking and squeezes me tighter as if she can't get close enough. Her sweet smell overwhelms me, causing me to bury my face into her neck, wanting more. "I'm just having a hard time right now."

"Me too, baby. Me too." Pulling away, I grab her chin and force a smile. "Take the day off. Let's both call in. I want to spend the day with you and see you smile. You need to smile."

There's no hesitation when she agrees to take the day off, and it makes my heart jump with joy. The old Tripp would never say no to an Alex and Tripp day. We need this more than we both know. "Where are we going?"

I tangle both of my hands into the back of her hair and massage. "Will you go see my mother with me? I just want to sit there like old times, in silence, just remembering all the good times. You're the only one that seems to soothe my pain when there and it's been a while since I've gone."

Her voice is thick with emotion when she responds. "Of course, Alex. I miss her too." She squeezes my hand and smiles. "I'm going to take a quick shower. Meet me by your truck in twenty?" She backs away with the cutest grin I've ever fucking seen. I love this girl.

"My truck in twenty." I flash my dimples and laugh as I watch her walk toward the door. "You know me well, Firecracker."

She stops and peers over her right shoulder. "I do. Never forget that." She winks and my dick twitches.

Seriously . . . just like that. Just like fucking that.

Just like always, when I walk outside twenty minutes later, fresh out of the shower, she's standing beside my truck looking painfully beautiful. She's wearing one of my favorite dresses today. The material is red, thin, and skin tight. It takes everything in me not to run my hands all over her stunning body and tell her that I want her for myself . . . to myself.

"You look hot." I lift my brows, making her burst into laughter as I check her out. "What? You do. That's my favorite dress on you. I've never denied it. You're definitely my firecracker now."

"Alright, stud." She tries to hide her face, but I still manage to see her face turn just about as red as that damn dress. I love that I can make her feel that good. She deserves to blush at least once every day, and I know for a fact that Lucas can't do that for her. "Let's go. Memphis and Lyric are meeting us there. They don't have much time before work."

My heart squeezes at the mention of her inviting my brother and Lyric. The things this woman does are so damn incredible, and she doesn't even have to try. It just comes naturally.

I smile at her, silently showing my appreciation before helping her into my truck.

When we arrive at the cemetery, Memphis and Lyric are already parked. Looking through the windshield for them, I spot them both sitting in the grass about fifteen feet away.

"Oh good." Tripp smiles and reaches over to squeeze my hand. "The whole family is here now. It's been too long since we've done this."

Tripp lets go of my hand and hops out of the truck. She looks back at me, but I give her the okay to go. I just need a small moment to myself. Seeing my mother's name etched across the tombstone never gets any easier. Not one fucking bit.

LIZZY CARTER
Loving Mother and fighter till the end.
You shall never be forgotten

Those words have haunted me for six years now.

Clenching my jaw to keep the tears at bay, I run my hands over my face and lean into the steering wheel. "Be strong for her. That's all she's ever wanted."

I wait a few minutes before finally getting out of the truck and joining the others.

Memphis instantly walks over and pulls me in for a hug, wrapping his arms around my head. "She's good, bro. She's happy and healthy. Remember that."

I slap his shoulder and squeeze it before pulling away. "I know, man. I'm just picturing her smile."

Memphis smiles and grips both of my shoulders. "I love that woman's smile. You were the lucky asshole that got her dimples. Lucky dick . . . "

Lyric pulls Memphis away and forces her way in between us. "My turn. Come here, Alex." She pulls me in for a tight hug and kisses my cheek. "It's good to see you." She leans in next to my ear and talks quietly. "I want to talk to you for a minute."

I look over Lyric's shoulder and see Memphis standing next to Tripp with his arm around her shoulder. It makes me happy to see how close they've grown since he's gotten out of prison. That's another reason why I can't *fuck* this all up. "What's up?"

Grabbing my hand, she pulls me away so that we can talk privately. "I'm going to give you some advice and I hope you take it. Listen to me, Alex. I love you like a brother. You know that, right?"

I nod my head. "Yeah . . . of course. I love you too, girl."

My heart starts racing as she glances back over at Tripp. I know where this conversation is headed and I'm not sure that I can handle it right now. I'm already confused as shit.

"You love her, Alex. I can see it in everything that you do."

I nod my head. "Of course I do. That girl is everything to me. I breathe for her, but that's no secret."

She gives me a hard look and grabs my chin, forcing me to look her in the eyes. "Tell me what the hell you're going to do about that."

"What the fuck am I supposed to do, Lyric? She's my best fucking friend. There's nothing I can do about it. I'm not ruining thirteen years of friendship if it doesn't work out. I can't do that shit."

"After thirteen years you still question if it could work out? Make her yours before someone else does. That's what you do about it. Do you want to see her with someone else? Like really *see* her . . . Do you want Lucas to keep her to himself?"

"Fuck no." I clench my jaw in anger just thinking about Lucas touching her. "That motherfucker doesn't deserve her. Who enjoys sleeping with other women when they have a girl like Tripp? Don't even get me started on him right now."

"I know that, Alex. You don't have to tell me. I hear things. I know things. Every time that I talk to that woman she tells me how much she cares for you, how you made her smile that day, or that you made her breakfast . . . washed her apron, or whatever else you do for her. You're a good man, Alex. That woman lives to fucking make you happy and you live to make her happy. That's the only kind of true love there is. It wins out over everything. What you two have is the only relationship that *will* work."

She grabs the back of my head and places her forehead to mine. "It's time to cross that line and show her how you truly feel. You're important to me. I don't want to see you miserable, and I know for a fact that if you two don't speak up fast . . . that's what you'll be. Don't make me watch that, Alex. I need you happy. Memphis needs you happy. He worries about you."

Her words shake me up and I find myself staring at Tripp as she leans into Memphis' shoulder to cry. Fuck, it makes my heart ache. The only thing I can think about is getting to her as fast as I can and comforting her. I live to comfort her.

"Shit . . . I gotta take care of her. We'll talk later."

Walking up behind Tripp, I pull her away from Memphis and bury her against my chest. "It's okay, baby. Let it out."

"I miss her. I miss seeing you two together." She sniffles and wipes her face across my shirt. "You were always so happy when you were with her . . . and Memphis." She starts crying harder. "He didn't even get to be there for her last days. I don't know . . . It's just hitting me hard. I'm sorry."

"Don't ever be sorry for crying for my family. Don't ever be ashamed to cry in front of me. I want to see every side of you. I want it all," I say, being completely honest, and hoping that she doesn't figure out in which way I mean that.

She looks up from my chest a few seconds later and reaches out to wipe away my single tear. She's bawling her eyes out, yet she's worried about my one tear over her face that is now pouring enough to create a puddle.

Fuuuck . . . I love you. I'm in fucking love with you.

I want to say it aloud so damn bad, but stop myself before I do. She's already emotional enough, and I can't bear the thought of adding to it.

"Can we sit here for a while?"

I lean in and kiss under both of her wet eyes. "Absolutely."

Sitting down, I pull her down with me, positioning her between my legs and wrapping my arms around her. She leans her head back on my shoulder and we sit like this for a while, not speaking. We don't need to in this moment.

Memphis and Lyric stand beside us, holding each other for as long as they can before they have to say goodbye. Lyric makes sure to give me *that look,* before jumping into Memphis' car and driving off.

Tripp and I stay for another hour, just holding each other and remembering the good times. In this moment I love this woman more than the world. Even if I don't ever tell her I'm going to hold onto this feeling, in this exact moment, for the rest of my life.

This woman has always been my *something for the pain,* and losing her will feel like dying . . .

TWENTY-FIVE

TRIPP

AFTER LEAVING THE CEMETERY I called Dax to tell him that I wouldn't be making it into work today. It's the first time that I've called off, and I honestly don't regret it. Dax has worked my ass off over the last week and I deserve a little time off, dammit. I want my time with Alex, especially since it could be ending soon. Alex will always come first to me and I don't care what anyone says. Today was more than worth it.

We spent a couple of hours this morning at Tara's house, visiting my aunt before she had to run off to work. She made sure to put Alex to work before making us her special brownies and telling us about some guy named Lance she met last week at work. She tried to pretend he was nobody special, but she let it slip that she's hoping he noticed her new and hip haircut.

Alex made sure to compliment her about fifteen times on her new do before we left, sending her off to work in the best mood I've possibly ever seen her in over the course of my damn life.

After leaving my aunt's we spent the next few hours hanging out in Alex's room while he sat back on his special chair and played the guitar, singing random songs that I would yell out at him. Watching him play brought a smile to my face, reminding me of a time before things got complicated. He looked so happy and at peace sitting there with that guitar in his arms that I never wanted to pull him out of the zone he was in; but of course, in typical Alex fashion, when he noticed me getting tired he pulled me onto his bed, buried me into his chest, and we both somehow fell asleep while talking about his mom and brother back when things were happy and good. It made me sad to never get to see them that way.

It's now well past six and I wake up to an empty bed, feeling somewhat lost that Alex somehow managed to slip away from me. Apparently . . . it's that easy. That reminder is unsettling.

I sit up and run my hands over my face, before groaning when a sick feeling hits me. I always feel like crap after waking from a nap. It's like the little bit of sleep that I get is just a tease for my body and now my body is being a bitch about it. It's such a shitty feeling.

Not knowing where Alex is, I hop out of bed and walk into the bathroom to find him completely naked and sitting in the tub. It's filled with very little water, not leaving much to the imagination.

His muscles are flexed, his tattooed flesh dripping with water as he leans back with his arms resting on the sides of the tub.

In this moment he's so damn sexy that I'm at a complete loss for words. I've never seen something so damn beautiful in my life, and all I can think about is him fucking me, slow and deep in that tub, and not stopping until we're both out of breath and unable to move.

Why does he have to be so tempting? Mmm . . . I want him so damn bad right now, every inch of him.

Alex pulls me out of my thoughts by sitting up and reaching for my arm, pulling me down into the hot water with him. "Come here."

I hiss a little from the heat on my flesh as the water soaks into my clothing. "Alex . . . what are you doing?"

He manages to roll us both over until he's hovering above me, his muscles flexing as he holds himself up. "If you're going to watch me like that . . . then you better be prepared to get wet."

He sucks my bottom lip into his mouth and gently bites it. I close my eyes when I feel his hand grip my thigh and squeeze. "You love me getting you wet? Don't you, babe?"

Moaning, I nod my head and close my eyes again when I feel his fingers move across my clit. It feels like heaven.

Everything he does feels too good to be true. "Alex don't . . ." He starts moving faster, causing me to shake below him, and trying to get a grip before I—"I'm going to come if you don't . . . Ahhh . . . Alex . . . ahhhhhh."

He smiles in satisfaction as I come undone below him, digging my nails into his bare flesh. "Fuck yes. I could listen to that sound every day for the rest of my life."

His face takes on a dark expression, as if he just said something that he didn't mean to, before he runs his hands over his face and stands up to reach for a towel. "I should get dressed and start setting the back yard up for the party."

I nod my head, fighting to catch my breath as I watch his muscles flex with each move that he makes while he wraps the towel tightly around his waist. "Yeah . . . okay. That's a good idea. I'll be down in a bit."

"No rush, babe. I have to run to the store anyways." His eyes roam over my wet body once, before stopping on my tits. He runs his tongue over his lips, wetting them. "Shit . . . "

And just like that he disappears into his room, leaving me craving more. Having him touch me like that and not feeling him deep inside me, filling me, is like taking my will to breathe away. I feel like a total mess right now.

I sit in the bathtub, not wanting to move for a good twenty minutes, before finally draining the water and taking a quick shower, hoping to clear my head.

All I can manage to think about is the last time I was in this shower with Alex making love to me. This has all become too overwhelming for me. I'm trying, but I can't put

Alex back into the friend zone. Not wanting to touch him is almost as hard as not breathing. I'm starting to feel as if I need him to survive. This is exactly what I *didn't* want to happen.

Feeling completely out of it, I get dressed and quickly do my hair and makeup, before heading downstairs to search through the cupboards for snacks and drinks that we have on hand. Surprisingly we still have a shit ton of alcohol sitting around. I really don't know why Alex felt he needed to go to the store.

Alex shows up sometime during my search, setting five plastic bags down onto the kitchen island. "I got a bunch of shit for tonight." He pulls out a bag of Mesquite BBQ Krunchers. "Your favorite chips for one." Then he pulls out five more bags and tosses them down, watching me with a smile.

I laugh when I notice that's the only type of chips he got; every single bag. "Did you really only buy my favorite chips?"

"Yeah." He shrugs his shoulders as if it isn't a big deal. "If we run out I will just buy you some more. We're also going to be serving a shitload of these motherfuckers tonight." He winks and flashes me his playful dimples, before pulling out a bunch of stuff to make Daiquiris.

I laugh even harder, totally pleased that he went to the store just to make sure that I had my favorite things. "You seriously couldn't be a better friend." Without thinking, I wrap my arms around his neck and crush my lips to his, moaning as he runs his tongue over my parted lips.

It happened so fast and came so naturally that I didn't even realize I started it until a throat clears beside us, bringing me back to reality.

We both pull away—well I pull away—and turn beside us to see Harley pulling up a stool. She grabs for a bag of my chips and opens them, popping one into her mouth as if nothing unusual just happened.

"Hey, y'all." She pops a few more chips into her mouth and talks while chewing. "These are damn good. I haven't had these since the last time you stayed at my house." She looks at the kitchen island. "Oh good. There's more. I'm eating this whole damn bag."

Alex sucks his bottom lip into his mouth and releases it, before smiling at me and backing out of the kitchen. "Enjoy, ladies. I'll be out back."

Harley and I both stare at each other in silence until Alex is out of earshot.

I break first, panicking. "Fuck me."

"Maybe later," she responds. "I'm holding out for Ace tonight. Mind if I use your room?"

"No!" I yell. "Gross . . ." I grab the bag of chips from her and toss them aside when she continues to pop them into her mouth, chewing as if there's no tomorrow. "I can't stop, Harley. I just kissed him without a second thought, as if he's my fucking boyfriend. That is not good. Not good at all."

"It looked pretty good to me, and it definitely fucking looked good for him too." She stands up and helps me shove the bags of ice into the freezer. "If I hadn't walked in that boy was going to bend you over that kitchen island and fuck you into oblivion." She points toward the back door. "He walked out that back door with a raging fucking hard-on. You're not the only one that can't stop. So why bother? Why stop?"

I slam the freezer door shut and grip my hair in frustration. "Because we're supposed to be best friends. That's why. We're supposed to be able to come to each other for anything and everything. We're supposed to be able to talk to each other, give each other advice, and look out for each other. Giving in and trying could ruin all of that if it doesn't work out. I can't lose him, Harley. You know that."

Harley looks at me as if I'm stupid. Her face stays blank for a few seconds, before she breaks into a sad smile. "Well apparently I'm the only one that can see this for what it really is; that you guys are made for each other. You two fuckers are damn blind if you ask me." She grips my shoulders and shakes me, as if to wake my ass up. "You will *never* lose him. Listen to my words. Never. Alex couldn't leave you if he wanted to."

I tilt my head up to meet her eyes. "Why?"

Harley smiles as if she has the only answer I need. "Because he's in love with you." The doorbell rings. Harley gets excited and releases my shoulders. "Now let's party."

EVER SINCE MY CONVERSATION WITH Harley, I haven't been able to keep my thoughts in check. How could she say what she did? How could she get my hopes up that Alex could possibly be *in love* with me? It only confuses me even more? She's a shitty friend . . . at least right now, and she is definitely not using my damn room. She can get laid in Ace's shitty old car.

Everyone around me is partying, drinking, playing games, and doing who knows what, yet here I am sitting on the edge of the pool, dipping my legs inside, and just trying to get lost into my own little world.

I feel bad, especially after Alex took the time to take a trip to the store, but I just can't get my head into having fun.

Random people, a few cute guys included, have sat down next to me in an attempt to get me hyped up, but once they figure out that I'm not interested in anything but sitting here and moping, they take off to find someone that actually knows how to have fun.

I look up from the water and see Alex entertaining a group of people by the bonfire. He's talking to them, holding conversations, and catching the attention of every girl around him, yet I catch him looking my way every few minutes.

I smile at him when I catch him looking again, but instead of smiling back he clenches his jaw as if he's bothered. I instantly feel like shit that I'm most likely ruining his fun and possibly even his game. I'm sure me sitting here like a loner is holding him back.

Jumping to my feet, I grab my drink and get ready to make my way inside, but as soon as I make it to the door I feel a hand grab mine and pull me.

I spin around to see Alex giving me a hard look. "Where are you going?"

"I'm not really up for partying. I'm going to my room."

I try to pull my hand from his grip and walk away, but Alex squeezes my hand tighter. "Stay with me." His jaw flexes as his eyes lock with mine. "I want you with me." He tilts his head toward the fire. "Let's go, babe."

Not able to say no to Alex, I begin walking along with him. I notice that we're still holding hands and attempt to pull away, but he grabs my hand tighter, lacing his strong fingers with mine. I look down at his tattooed hand holding mine and my heart swells. It's a beautiful sight and I want it . . . *forever.*

He doesn't release my hand, even when we get lost in the crowd surrounding the fire. His thumb begins to gently rub mine as if trying to relax me. I appreciate the gesture, but all it does is wind me up tighter, making me want him even more.

"Play a song, Alex." An attractive blonde appears next to Alex and claps her hands excitedly. Her smile falters when she looks down to see his hand entwined with mine. That definitely doesn't please her.

She has a fresh tattoo of a tree on her ribcage and it doesn't take a genius to see that it's Alex's work. It's fucking beautiful and so is she. It makes my heart hurt so bad that it stops for a second.

I catch Alex off guard, yanking my hand away from his. "Yeah, good idea."

He tilts his head to the side and clenches his jaw as if aggravated at me that I pulled away. "Give me a minute, Divinity." His voice is a little harsher than usual, but it doesn't seem to faze the girl.

The cute blonde just smiles flirtatiously at him and then does this little ass shake as she walks back over to join her group of girls.

"Are you okay?" Alex grabs my hand and stops me from twirling my ring. "I don't like seeing you like this."

He smiles when I don't answer. "I wrote a song. You know I can't write for shit, but I'm going to sing it anyway." He starts backing away to his guitar. "And I better see a damn smile on that beautiful face when I'm done."

A small smile tries to take over as he reaches for his guitar and takes a seat on one of the tree trunks, but I force it back. I don't want to cave too soon, especially when he hasn't even played anything yet.

Everyone starts clapping as he plays this fun little tune that I've never heard. He stops in the middle of it and takes a swig of his beer, before playing again.

Everyone quiets down and listens as he starts to sing.

"It's been a while since I've known you, but it will never be too long.

A lot has happened, yet you've always stuck around.

From that day of pain I was deadened and frail, wandering along on a never ending trail.

Meaningless quests were the rules of my game, then I had a taste of you . . . and since—I haven't been the same.

I'm breathing you in, it's tearing me down.

My breaths become shaky and slightly rundown.

But it's okay, 'cause I don't want to be saved.

This pain inside is a part of you I crave. Burning slow, lighting a fire within, but it's alright because I'm still breathing, breathing you in.

I was supposed to protect you from guys like me but you're the only girl that can fulfill my needs.

You're my little red firecracker . . . "

He repeats this a couple of times, my heart beating so damn fast that I have to hold my chest to keep it from bursting through. His words, his mouth, his voice . . . so damn beautiful that it hurts.

He may think that he can't write for shit, but to me his words are the most beautiful that I've ever heard before, because they came from him.

Little red firecracker . . .

I don't even realize when the song ends, because I'm still lost in my own little world, slightly insane and imagining that the song could possibly be about me. I'm sure he just added the firecracker part to put me in a better mood, or I'm just giving it a double meaning when in fact it would be no different than him singing it to another friend. Those are the only reasonable explanations.

Whatever the reason, I'm smiling so big that it hurts.

Alex appears next to me, grabbing my chin and tilting it up. "There we go. There's that fucking smile that I needed." He throws his arm around me and pulls me against his side.

"Now let's enjoy this night, firecracker."

I try to speak, but every time I look at him I smile even bigger, unable to contain it, so I just nod my head and quickly ask for a drink.

I might need a few of those Daiquiris now . . .

TWENTY-SIX

ALEX

I CAN'T WRITE FOR SHIT and I know my song was crap, but it put a smile on her face and that's all that matters to me. That damn song is probably the closest that I'll get to being able to tell her how I truly feel. I threw it together in fifteen minutes, so there's more that I wanted to say, but didn't.

The party is coming to an end now, and seeing her relaxed and having fun with Harley makes me so fucking happy. I can't stop smiling like an idiot as I watch them dancing together and laughing.

"Dude . . ." Ace appears next to me, tilting back his drink. "You've got it bad, man."

I don't even bother denying it this time, because even

a blind person can see how much I love that girl. "I do . . . really fucking bad."

Ace smiles and turns his attention to the girls. "Harley is looking damn beautiful tonight."

I nudge his shoulder. "Then why the hell aren't you over there, bro?"

He finishes off his drink and crushes the cup. "Because I'm not good enough for her." It's the first honest, sincere thing that I've heard out of his mouth since I've known him.

I finish off my own drink and squeeze his shoulder. "Then learn to be . . . "

With that, I walk away wishing that I could do the same. I may not be able to give Tripp everything that she needs, but for tonight, I can give her me.

Ace takes my lead and makes his way over to Harley once I pull Tripp away and start leading her inside. The party can find its way out.

Tripp wraps her arms around me as soon as we close the door behind us. "I feel like swimming." She grips my shirt and starts pulling me toward the pool room. "Let's swim, Alex."

I watch her as she quickly strips down to her bra and panties, turns around to smile at me, and then jumps into the water, splashing me.

"Come on . . . get those clothes off and join me, Stud."

I smirk and pull my shirt over my head. "You know how I like to swim, babe." I toss my shirt aside and start undoing my jeans. "I never swim with clothes on."

She bites her bottom lip and reaches behind her to undo her bra. "No clothes . . . and just the two of us."

"Fuck me, Tripp. Swimming will never be the same."

She slips off her panties and tosses them out of the pool as I step out of my briefs, hard as a fucking rock for her. "That's what I'm counting on," she breathes out in a soft tone.

Not bothering to hide my erection, I walk into the pool, grabbing Tripp's face as soon as she's within reach. I press my forehead against hers and slip my hands into her hair, gripping it. "Do you want me inside you, baby?" I suck her bottom lip into my mouth, before releasing it. "You want me to make love to you? I want to so fucking bad right now, but I won't unless you tell me you want it."

She swallows hard and wraps her arms around my neck, pulling herself up to wrap her legs around my waist. "I want you to make love to me." She presses her forehead to mine, before sinking down onto my cock. "I love you inside of me. I need it."

With those words I wrap my arms around her and slowly start lifting her up and down on my dick, being sure to sink deep into her with each thrust.

Our touches become desperate, our kisses deep and passionate, as if this is the last moment that we get to be together this way. That thought causes me to give her all of me, every inch of me physically and emotionally.

We make love for what seems like hours, me slowing down when needed to keep this moment from ending. I can go all fucking night, and that's exactly what I plan on doing. This woman deserves all of me, and that's what I'm giving her. I won't stop until she orgasms so many times she can't withstand anymore and is exhausted.

"Alex," she moans. "I'm about to come again. I can't . . . I can't." She grips onto me as tightly as she can, digging her nails into my back as we both release at the same time. "It's so sensitive." She shakes in my arms and jumps when I move a little bit inside of her, making sure that I'm as deep as I can get.

"Damn, baby . . ." I kiss her hard and deep, pulling her as close to me as I possibly can. "I love watching you come undone around me." I rub my thumb over her cheeks. "You're the most beautiful woman in the world to me, babe."

A tear slides down her cheek that I quickly wipe away with my thumb. "You mean that?" She questions with hope.

"I do," I whisper.

A few more tears slide down her cheek. Not knowing what's going to happen in the next couple days, I just hold her and comfort her. I hate to see her cry. I fucking hate it so damn much.

We stay like we are for a little while longer, before I walk us over to the shallow end and finally pull out of her. I'm surprised that I'm actually still somewhat hard, but I can't help it when it comes to her.

Setting her down, I help her out of the water and grab my shirt. "Come here, babe." I slip my shirt over Tripp's head, before reaching for the small towel that I left in here earlier, and slip it around my waist, tucking it.

"I'm hungry," Tripp says with a cute little smile. "Want some ice cream?"

I kiss the top of her head and smile. "Lead the way."

Once we get into the kitchen Tripp pulls out a tub of her favorite ice cream and grabs two spoons, digging one in and scooping out a spoonful. "Cookie dough okay? There's chocolate if you want something else."

Answering her question, I bend down and take her spoon in my mouth, sucking the ice cream off. "I'm having what you're having, babe."

She laughs as I bite her spoon and pull it out of her grip. "Alex . . . you're so damn cute that it's ridiculous."

I flash my dimples and playfully lift my brows at her, while removing the spoon from my mouth. "Who me? Should I apologize?"

She leans in and licks the side of my mouth. "No." She smiles. "You're messy too, by the way."

I suck my bottom lip into my mouth, getting what she missed. "I know . . . I did it on purpose."

Everything is perfect right now. This is what I can see myself doing for the rest of my fucking life, and never getting tired of being with her. I want this moment to last forever . . . but I know that's not an option. Or is it?

The back door opens and we both look over in shock as Lucas walks in and sets his suitcase down. He looks around at the messy kitchen. "Party night . . . I missed it. Shit."

My heart starts beating out of my chest as he walks

over and grabs Tripp's hand, pulling her up to her feet. An overwhelming feeling to kill this motherfucker takes over. I watch his every move as if my life depends on it.

"Lucas, what are you doing back so soon? I thought . . . "

Lucas cuts her off by crushing his lips to hers and cupping her right ass cheek, slipping his hand up *my* shirt as if she's his. Fuck him, because she's mine and she's in *my* fucking shirt.

I see red and lose my ability to fucking think straight.

Being careful not to hurt Tripp, I grab Lucas by the throat and slam him up against the wall. "Don't you fucking touch her, motherfucker." He attempts to pull away from me, so I grip him tighter, slamming him against the wall again, but harder this time.

"Alex!" I feel Tripp grip my shoulder and start pulling on it. "Stop! Please don't fight."

Catching me off guard, Lucas breaks free from the wall and shoves me, causing me to stumble backward into the kitchen island.

Out of instinct, I swing out, knocking him on his fucking ass.

He grabs for his jaw and looks up at me. "What the fuck is wrong with you? Are you insane, asshole?"

Before I can lose my shit, Tripp jumps in front of me and holds me back, afraid that I'll hurt him. She knows how I get when I fight. She's heard it all. "I said stop! Both of you."

I swallow hard and clench my jaw, trying my best to keep my cool. Seeing him put his hands on her hurt like hell. I never want to see that shit again. She comes before everyone. I could care less about my past with Lucas. He can fuck off.

Tripp looks back and forth between the two of us. Suddenly she starts breathing heavily as if she's having a panic attack. "I need to get out of here. Shit . . . I need to go. I just need to go."

She rushes out of the kitchen. Everything in me wants to go after her, but I don't want to do anything to trigger her even more. I couldn't handle it if something were to happen to her.

I look down at Lucas on the ground, before forcing myself to leave the kitchen. If I stay . . . I will hurt his ass.

I shove the back door open and fight to catch my breath. I never wanted Tripp to have to see me this way. I've always done my best to keep her away when I had fights. I always told her about them, but never let her watch.

"Fuuuck!"

I'm outside for less than three minutes when I hear Tripp's car start up and pull out of the driveway. My first instinct is to freak out, but I quickly stop myself. There's only one place she'd be going if she needed to get away, and that is Tara's.

I'll give her a little time to calm down and then we need to talk. I need to apologize and tell her how I feel.

I need to tell her that I'm in love with her . . .

TWENTY-SEVEN

ALEX

HAVING TRIPP WALK OUT THAT door has been one of the worst feelings of my entire life. I never thought I'd see the day that Tripp walked away from me, not wanting to be near me. It kills me, and I'm not afraid to admit that I can't handle it.

It's been four days now, and the longer that she's gone the more it causes an ache in my chest. It feels so heavy that it sometimes feels hard to breathe. I feel like a piece of me is missing. The problem is, I know exactly what that piece is, but that piece isn't ready to come back to me yet, and I'm afraid that forcing it will only push her further from my reach. I'm not willing to lose her forever.

I'm sitting at *Monty's* by myself, checking my phone

every few minutes to see if Tripp has responded to any of my messages yet. I asked her to meet me here so we could talk. It's the one place that I thought she'd agree to.

Looking down at my phone I notice that there's still no response, and my heart sinks for what seems like the millionth time since Tripp stormed away.

Slowly exhaling, I toss my phone into the wall beside me and run my hands through my hair, tugging. Suddenly, eating seems like the last thing I want to do, so I shove my plate aside, grab my cracked phone, and toss some cash on the table.

I've been sitting in that spot for three hours now and the disappointment that I feel can't be denied. I can't sit here anymore because it hurts too much. It's pretty clear that she doesn't want to see me right now.

Lost in hurt and anger at myself, as well as my idiotic decisions over the last few weeks, I drive home, grab my guitar, and play to myself for hours. It's my only for sure escape.

Every so often I look over as if expecting Tripp to be there, listening beside me, but she's not. I never thought there'd be a day that would happen, and I never want to feel the emptiness that it brings again.

I need to do something before it's too late. I know that now more than ever . . .

TRIPP

I LOOK DOWN AT MY PHONE for the fifth time in the last ten minutes. Seeing Alex's unanswered message causes an ache in my chest that I can't explain.

It kills me. I almost can't take it, but I know that if I cave and see him now, it's going to hurt way too much when we realize that we need to move on and put the last few weeks behind us. I'm not ready for that disappointment and I'm afraid that what's left of my heart will die.

Running my fingers over his message, I click reply and stop to stare at the screen. I stare at it for a while, trying to figure it out. How do I say no to Alex? How do I tell him that I'm not ready to lose him yet . . . or that I'm in love with him and can't live without him?

I don't. I can't, so I toss my phone aside and bury myself under the blanket, holding back the cries that have been burning in the back of my throat all day. It feels raw.

"I'm sorry," I say softly into the air. "So sorry."

I never meant to lose you . . .

TWENTY-EIGHT

ALEX

TRIPP HASN'T BEEN HOME IN eight days now. Eight fucking days! She hasn't been at work either. I've been texting her pretty much every hour for the last few days, but all she's been sending back are short, one worded answers. At least that's an improvement from before. I hate that she feels she has to do that with me. It just shows me how truly confused and stressed out she must be feeling at the moment. I want to fix that, but she's not giving me the chance right now, and I refuse to tell her something this important over a fucking text message.

Lucas just walked in the door from work or who the fuck knows where. We haven't spoken since that day and we have been working to avoid each other. He gets ready to walk into the kitchen but stops and grips the doorframe when he sees me standing shirtless, dripping with sweat.

I'm pretty sure he knows not to fuck with me right now.

"Tripp won't answer her phone still. Good job, shithead." He releases the doorframe and walks over to the fridge, pulling out a beer. "I've called her like ten damn times just today. Nothing. I have to hear her fucking voice on a recording."

I steel my jaw and pour my bottled water over my head, not having shit to say. I have to admit that I'm happy to hear that she's not answering for him.

He continues talking when he realizes that he's about to have a one-sided conversation. "I had a feeling there was more to your friendship all along, but I needed to know before things between Tripp and I became serious." He pauses to open his beer and tilt it back. He sets it down hard. "You might not believe it, but I love her too, dammit. I've given Tripp her damn space for the last twelve months, hoping that she would see me with other women and realize that she was ready to have me to herself. Not one time has she shown any kind of jealousy when it comes to me with another woman. Never."

I shake my wet hair and grip the counter.

"I was jealous as shit to see you two together, but I had to know if I was right about you two. I needed to know if she loved you, and after that night I know for a fact that she does. She doesn't love me, man. It sucks, but it's mostly my fault. I guess it's true what they say . . . Never let your girl have a male best friend."

I tilt my head his way. He's gripping his bottle so tightly that his knuckles are white.

"Alex fucking Carter," he grumbles. "You're the reason she was never ready in the first place. It was you that she was afraid of losing all along."

His words cause my heart to ache. What if he's right? What if she has been waiting all these years for me and I was the idiot, trying my best to keep myself from falling. I'm a fucking asshole.

Shit, Tripp . . . I'm an idiot.

I push away from the counter and look up at the clock to see that it's past ten. Tara is probably in bed, ready to get up early for work in the morning. I need to see Tripp. Tonight.

I give Lucas one last look before gripping my shirt, throwing it on, and running out the door.

My truck is in reverse and pulling out of the driveway before I can fully think it through. This is something that needs to be said in person, and the idea of making her wait any longer is killing me.

All of the lights are off when I arrive in front of Tara's house. Just like in the past, I jog over to the side of the house and reach for Tripp's window to open it. I push up, but it doesn't move.

"Fuck."

She never locks her window. My stomach sinks and I find myself gripping my hair in frustration. I need to get to her and it seems as if she's doing what she can to keep me away.

A feeling of pain so deep rushes through me that I have the urge to punch something, but I don't. I can't lose my temper.

I glance over at Tara's window and see that it's opened a crack. Without a second thought, I push her window open and shove my leg through it.

Tara quickly sits up from bed and whisper yells my name once I get fully inside. "Alex!" She rubs her hands over her face and shakes her head at me. "It's called the front door. The key is on your ring. It has been for years now. Give the window a rest and let me get *my* rest."

I rush over to Tara, grab her head, and kiss the top of it. "Sorry, Tara. I need to see Tripp."

Tara gives me an understanding look and smiles tiredly at me. "I'm glad you're here," she whispers. "Now get out of here. I have a lunch date tomorrow and I need all the beauty rest I can get."

I grin at her. "Nah . . . you don't need any." Then I quickly rush out the bedroom door, making my way next door to Tripp's room.

I stop and take a deep breath, before pushing her door open and stepping inside.

She's sitting up on her bed, looking straight at me when I enter, as if she's been waiting.

"Your window was locked," I say gently.

She pulls her eyes away from me, and huffs. "I know. I just needed a little more time alone." She jumps to her feet and throws her arms up. "I'm so fucking confused right now. I'm filled with so many emotions that I can't figure out how to breathe. I feel like I'm suffocating, Alex. I can't fucking breathe," she cries.

I reach out to touch her face, but she turns away from me. It fucking kills me. "Tripp . . . we need to talk. I need to tell you—"

"Alex," she cuts me off. "Can we wait until tomorrow? I just need tonight to really get all my thoughts together before I say or do something that I might regret for the rest of my life. I want you here . . ." She turns around and our eyes meet. I hate the pain I see in hers, but I have a feeling that mine are reflecting the same. "But it might not be the best right now. A lot has happened over the weeks. I think we both need this right now. I'm scared. So damn scared. Please understand."

It hurts like hell, but I respect her with everything in me, and if she needs another night I will give it to her, but one night is all I'm willing to give. "Okay," I whisper. I pull her into my arms and hold her for what feels like forever. My heart feels like it's beating again for the first time in eight days. Then I kiss the top of her head, like I always do. "After I get off work tomorrow. I don't need any more time to think. I know what I want and I'm coming to find you the minute I walk out that damn door."

Pulling away, she looks up at me as I back away from her. "I'm not working tomorrow. I'm going with Tara on her lunch date and then I'm coming back here. I'll be ready to talk. I promise."

I nod my head and walk away before I can lose it and tell

her everything that I'm dying to say right now. I gently close her door behind me, careful not to disturb Tara anymore tonight.

It's going to be a bitch to get through work tomorrow . . .

TWENTY-NINE

ALEX

"YO, DUDE. WHAT THE FUCK?" The skater-looking dude with blue hair that I've been working on pulls his arm away and sits up. "Do you need a break or something? You're in a zombie zone or some shit. Don't fuck my shit up."

I take a deep breath and pull his arm back to its original position, not giving a shit if I piss him off at this point. "Hold still," I say stiffly.

I swear if I don't get out of here soon, I'm going to fucking lose it. I've been in this damn room for the last three hours, when all I really want to do is be in whatever room Tripp is.

I get distracted when my phone vibrates across the desk. It's the second time in the last three minutes, and with each time I get more anxious, wondering if it's Tripp.

"You need to get that, dude?"

Flexing my jaw, I set the gun down and pull my gloves off. "Give me a minute."

"Whatever gets your head back in the game, bro. I'm going outside for a smoke."

My heart skips a beat when I pick up my cell to see Tripp's name flash across the screen. This is now the third time. That doesn't sit well with me.

With my heart racing, I answer it. "Tripp, is everything—"

"Hello," A voice that isn't Tripp's interrupts me. "Is this Alex?"

Feeling as if my hearts going to beat out of my chest, I grip the desk. "What the fuck is going on? Where's Tripp?"

The girl on the other end is silent for a few seconds, causing my anxiety to grow.

"Answer me," I growl into the phone. "Please."

"I'm sorry. Your friend was involved in a car accident." My heart fucking stops as she continues. "I found her phone in the car and dialed the last person that she talked to. She's being loaded into the ambulance as we speak. I think she may need you."

"Fuck!" I start shaking as I reach for my keys and run out the door, still holding the phone. "Text me the name of which hospital they are taking her to."

I shove the door open and rush past my client, not bothering to stop as he questions where the fuck I'm going.

All I can think about is losing Tripp. I can't lose her. It's taking everything in me right now not to break down and fucking cry. This is my worst nightmare. I need to get to her.

Not even a minute of being on the road and the message comes from Tripp's phone telling me the name of which hospital she's at.

Slamming down on the gas pedal, I drive as fast as I can for as long as I can, until traffic slows me down, bringing me to a complete stop.

"Fucking get out of my way!" I turn on my emergency flashers and punch the horn repeatedly, knowing damn well that it's not going to do shit to get me there sooner.

Looking around me, I try to back out of traffic, but other cars start piling up behind me, blocking me in. This is when I really start to lose it.

"Fuck this . . . "

Opening my door, I jump out of my truck and start running, weaving my way through traffic. Cars start honking and yelling at me when they realize that I'm leaving my truck there, but I could care less. I think I even jumped over one of the cars. I can't be sure, because everything is in a haze.

I run fifteen blocks, not stopping once to catch my breath, not even when I get to the hospital. Fuck my lungs. Fuck the pain burning in my chest. All I care about is getting to my woman.

Rushing inside, I grip the desk and yell out Tripp's name. "Tripp Daniels!" I fight to catch my breath as the woman starts typing her name into the computer. "Hurry!" I yell, getting impatient.

"I'm sorry, sir." The woman looks up from the computer.

"Her name is not listed here. I checked twice."

I slam my fist down, starting to lose my shit even more. "Check again."

The woman swallows and gives me a sympathetic look. "I understand your worry, sir, but I can assure you her name is not listed."

Cursing to myself, I run my hands up and down my sweaty face, before putting my thoughts together. I remember her saying she was going on a lunch date with Tara today. "Can you please check for Tara Daniels?"

The woman nods her head and starts typing into the computer again. "Yes, sir. Tara is here, but you have to be family to go back. What is your name?"

"Shit!" I grip my hair, knowing that this isn't going to go well. I need to get the fuck back there. "Alex Carter," I say stiffly.

The woman smiles and then presses a button. "She's in room 107. It's going to be on—"

Before she can finish I rush through the door and start running like a fucking crazy person. Someone stops walking to yell at me to slow down, but I ignore him.

I stop to take a deep breath when I reach room 107, before poking my head around the curtain to see Tara sitting up and watching TV.

Her eyes widen in surprise when she sees me. "Alex, how did you know I was here?"

I walk over to the side of her bed and grab her hand. "Fuck, you're okay. Where's Tripp? Is she hurt? Tell me!"

Tara gives me a confused look and squeezes my hand. "Tripp is fine. She's at work. She got asked to cover a shift."

Relief washes over me and I pull Tara in for the biggest hug of her life. I'm squeezing her so tightly that I'm almost afraid of hurting her, but she doesn't seem to be in pain.

"Alex." She runs her hand over my forehead after we pull away. "Are you feeling well? I'm so damn confused right now."

I shake my head and grab the chair behind me, pulling it up next to the bed. "Some woman called me from Tripp's phone and said she was in an accident, so I got here as fast as I could."

"Shit." Tara takes a deep breath and relaxes into her bed. "She must've left her phone in my car. Dax called her when we were on the way to my lunch date so I dropped her off at the bar."

I smile. "I'm sorry. I'm not happy that you're here, but I'm sure as fuck happy to hear that Tripp is okay." I stand up and reach for my cell. "I'll call Tripp at work and let her know what happened."

"No." Tara shakes her head. "I'm fine. They just want to run a few tests before sending me home. I don't want to distract Tripp while she's at work."

I put my phone away and take a seat again, reaching for a magazine.

"What are you doing?" Tara asks with a small smile.

"Staying here." I throw my leg up and get comfortable. "I'm not leaving you here alone, Tara."

Tara looks at me lovingly, making me feel as if I truly am family. "You're a good guy, Alex. I love you like family. You know that right?"

I smile and close the magazine. "I kind of figured that when my name was on the list of family for visitors. I love you too, Tara. You're like the aunt I never had."

THEY RAN A COUPLE TESTS on Tara and finally released her a couple hours later. After getting her comfortable on the couch, I make her the lunch that she never got to eat and leave her to relax.

I recovered Tripp's phone from the hospital and shoved it in my pocket with mine. It's so weird wanting to talk to her, but knowing that her phone is with me. I can't remember a time that we haven't texted each other through work.

It looks like my only option is to *see* her at work. I just need to make a quick stop first.

I just hope that she's ready for me . . .

THIRTY

TRIPP

EVERYTHING IN ME WISHES THAT I would have told Dax no when he asked me to come in today. I have too much on my mind and I've been messing up most of the orders since I walked through that door; mixing the wrong drinks or even forgetting to make them completely. I'm a complete mess right now, not to mention that I forgot my phone in Tara's car. That never happens, confirming just how messed up I am.

I keep wanting to check it to see if Alex has texted me, but every time I go to reach for it by the register, I have to remind myself that it's not there. I may be too mixed up to think straight or even talk to Alex right now, but seeing his messages come through calms me unlike anything else in this world can.

I know we need to talk later. There's so much that needs to be figured out, but I'm terrified. I'm so terrified that my chest hurts.

Lucas and I are done; that I know for sure, and I'm okay with it. It was never meant to be in the first place. It's where Alex and I stand that scares the living shit out of me. I keep replaying this stupid made up conversation in my head, where I confess to Alex that I'm madly in love with him and he tells me that we can never be more than friends. The more I play it in my head, the more it begins to feel like reality; a reality that I don't want.

"Hey! Hey!" Dax snaps his fingers at me. "Did you get that order? Get it together, Tripp."

"I got it, Dax." I snap. "Just go. You're messing me up." I usher him out from behind the bar and he gives me a hard look, then stands by the end of the bar watching me, to make sure I *really have it.*

Luckily I manage to actually have it this time. The last thing I want to deal with right now is Dax riding my ass because I messed up again.

Finally, an hour later, it calms down enough for me to get a glass of soda and breathe for a minute.

"Hey, sweets."

I look beside me and smile as Harley leans in next to me and nudges my shoulder. "Hey, lady."

I try to act as if everything is okay, but by the look on Harley's face I can tell that I'm giving my true feelings away.

"I'm sorry, sweets." She rests her head on my shoulder. "I would tell you again that everything will be okay, but I know you're not looking to hear it from me."

"Thank you," I whisper. "At least I'll still have you by my side when this is all over."

Harley pushes my arm. "Oh stop it. You're depressing me with that talk. Alex isn't going anywhere. I promise . . . but like I said, you don't want to hear it from me."

"Yeah . . ." I admit. "I won't believe it until it comes from Alex. I guess I'll know once I actually get out of this stupid place."

I reach for my glass and get ready to refill my soda when I hear it: *This Year's Love* by David Gray. It sounds like it's coming from across the room.

My breath hitches in my throat and I drop my glass, watching it shatter next to my feet. I know for a fact that it's not the radio, because the radio has been turned down all day.

The sound gets closer, and the next thing I know I'm fighting for air as I turn around to see Alex with his guitar, walking straight for me.

He looks like a sexy, sinful dream come true . . . with his ripped up jeans and guitar, all tatted up. I have forgotten how to breathe at this point, and my heart leaps straight out of my chest as he gets closer.

Everyone around us quiets down and watches Alex as he drops down on one knee and starts singing the beginning Lyrics.

Tears begin to stream down my face as I watch him looking at me, as if he's going to break down and cry himself. His jaw keeps flexing and his hands are shaking, but his eyes never leave mine as he continues to sing in front of the whole bar.

Girls all around me start to gather and swoon as Alex motions with his head for me to come to him.

Slowly, I force my feet to work and walk around the bar. As soon as I get close enough to Alex, he stands up and grabs my face, singing to me without any music from his guitar.

Singing, he presses his forehead to mine and starts rubbing his thumbs over my face, wiping my tears away. I start to cry more as he swings his guitar behind him and wraps his arms around me, moving us both to the music.

"Is this really happening? Alex . . ." I whisper into his chest.

I can't believe this is happening right now. I feel as if any second now I'm going to wake up from this perfect moment and be standing here in this stupid bar, wishing that I were with Alex.

He whispers the last word to the song, before cupping my face and pressing his lips to mine. His kiss is so intense . . . so desperate and full of need that I almost die right here in his perfect arms: the perfect kiss of death.

His breath fans against my lips when he pulls away. "I love you, Tripp. I'm so fucking in love with you that I need you to breathe. I've been in love with you since the first day we met and every day with you only makes me love you more and realize that I *never* want to go another day without you. You are and will always be the best thing in my life and I promise to never let you forget that. I need to know that you love me too." He pulls my chin up and looks me in the eyes, before whispering," Do you?"

My eyes search his and I forget how to speak as he watches me, waiting for an answer. My grip on him tightens as I finally get my mouth to work. "You have no idea. I love you so much that I can't even breathe right now." I hold a shaky hand up. "I'm shaking right now because I never thought this day would come. You're my best friend and my whole world. I never want to lose you. I can't lose you. I need to know that I never will."

He tangles his hands into the back of my hair and moves his body into mine. "You will never lose me, Tripp. I just need to know one thing?" He runs his thumb over my bottom lip, taking my breath away. "Can I keep you? I don't just mean for today or for a week or a month. I need to know that I can keep you forever. I need you to be my something for the pain for the rest of my life."

He surprises me by dropping down to one knee and pulling a ring out of his pocket. "Tripp Hazel Daniels, will you be my wife? I want to marry you and make you smile every day for the rest of my life. I can't imagine a life without you and I definitely don't want to imagine your life without me in it. Say yes . . ." He whispers the last part and that's when I lose it.

I drop down to my knees in front of him and place a hand

over my mouth as the sobs start to escape. "Yes. Yes, Alex. A million times . . . yes! Every day for the rest of my life . . . yes." I nod my head continuously as the tears run down my face, soaking the front of my shirt.

I can barely even see the ring when Alex slips it on my finger, and I truly don't care. It could be a vending machine ring for all I care. All that matters to me is spending the rest of my life with my best friend: my future husband.

The bar erupts into cheers when Alex pulls me into his arms and kisses me. I can hear Harley happily crying above us and jumping around in excitement.

"Can I take you home? I've missed you so damn much."

I nod my head and laugh through the tears. "Yes, please. I need to get out of here."

"Good." Alex pulls me up to my feet and sucks my bottom lip into his mouth, biting it playfully, before releasing it. "Because I have eight days to make up to my fiancé." He smiles big, flashing his dimples. "Fuuck . . . I love the way that sounds."

I throw my arms around him and kiss him so hard that he almost falls backward into the bar. He grabs the back of my neck and smiles when we break the kiss. "Damn, baby. Now I really can't wait to get you home."

Harley throws her arms around me the second that she sees an opening. "I knew it!" She squeals. "I so knew it. Now get out of here. It's slow enough now. Dax can fuck off."

"I love you," I say thankfully. "Thank you, Harley."

Grabbing me by the back of the neck, Alex pulls me in for

a long kiss, before grabbing my hand and leading me out of the bar.

I can't stop smiling as I look at our hands entwined together. Everything about it just feels so right.

"I love it too," Alex says, pulling our hands up to kiss mine. "So get used to this; every fucking day. I am your man and I promise you I will show you that in every possible way."

"You're perfect, Alex. Seriously perfect," I admit.

Alex pins me against his truck and spreads my legs with his thigh, making me straddle it. "I'm only perfect with you, babe." He kisses me soft and deep, before stopping and smiling against my lips. "I love you, Firecracker."

I moan as he pushes his thigh further between my legs, breathing heavily against my lips. "I love you." I lean my head back. "So damn much."

Alex removes his thigh from between my legs and smiles. "I'm going to love hearing that for the rest of my life." He bites his bottom lip seductively. "I want to get you home, but we have a stop to make first. I'll explain on the way."

Grabbing my ass, he helps me into his truck and rushes over to the other side. He starts his truck and hands me my phone. "Why don't you give Tara a call and tell her we're on the way."

I swallow hard, beginning to worry that something bad happened, but knowing Alex, he would be freaking out a lot more than he is if it had. It instantly calms me, letting me know that everything will be okay.

Alex always makes everything okay, and now I have the

chance to show him that for the rest of my life. Tripp Carter
. . . I love the sound of that, and I couldn't imagine it any
other way.

THIRTY-ONE

ALEX

TODAY IS MY BIRTHDAY AND all I want to do is get out of this shop, away from Ace and Styles' annoying asses, and spend the night with my wife. I just got done with my last appointment for the day and I can't deny that I rushed my way through it, being careful not to fuck up James' back piece in the process. He picked a shitty day to set an appointment anyway.

"Damn, birthday boy in a hurry today or what?" Styles jumps up to sit on the desk, watching me as I throw my leather jacket on. "Where you going anyway? No more appointments today?"

I grin at him as I reach for my keys. "*Monty's.* I'm meeting Tripp, Lyric, and Memphis for dinner and then I'm taking my wife home to pamper the shit out of her. I canceled my last appointment." I spin my keys around my finger. "That woman loves me, man. I'm the luckiest guy in the world. So yeah . . . I'm in a hurry. Everything else can wait."

Styles crosses his arms over his chest and looks over at Ace as he pops his head out of his room.

"Happy birthday, fucker." Ace shouts, before slapping the door and disappearing.

I turn to leave, giving Styles a quick head nod. "I'm out, man. Tell Ace I said to fuck off and have a good day."

"Alright, dude. Eat some good shit for me. I'm starving and there isn't shit for food around here. I need a nice, fat, juicy burger right now. That or some hot chick to walk through that door and that doesn't happen much these days since you scared them all away with that wedding ring."

"Yeah . . ." I nod my head and reach for the door. "Good luck, man."

Before Styles can hold me back any longer, I rush out the door and jog over to my truck, hopping inside to head to *Monty's*.

It's been eight months since I've asked Tripp to marry me, and three months since I've been able to call her my wife. Everything has changed since that day and I wouldn't go back to my old life for anything.

Styles and Ace may not be too excited about the lack of girls at the shop since I've been wearing this ring, but I haven't ever been happier in my entire life, and I make sure to tell them that daily when their asses are moping around complaining.

Since we got married Tripp and I have been going through the process of buying a house together, and we're supposed to hear word any day now. I'm hoping that Tripp will have some good news for me tonight at dinner. That shit would make my birthday complete.

I pull up outside of *Monty's* and practically jump out of my truck before I can even pull the keys out. It's been seven hours since I have tasted Tripp's lips, and right now that's the only thing I'm hungry for.

When I walk inside, I spot Tripp sitting across a table from my brother and Lyric. Memphis notices me first, whistling and yelling. "Over here, birthday boy."

I see Tripp twisting her wedding ring on her finger when I approach, but she quickly stops and jumps up to give me a kiss. "Happy birthday, stud."

I grab her face and kiss her harder when she tries taking a seat. "I don't think so, baby." I run my thumb over her lips and bite my own. "I haven't tasted those sweet lips all day. Come here."

She smiles against my lips as I kiss her for a third time. "I missed you too," she says, knowingly.

"Happy birthday, handsome," Lyric says happily as Tripp and I scoot into the booth. "You look nice today."

"Thanks, sis." I wink and reach for Tripp's hand, kissing it. "You guys ready to order yet? I already know what I want and I'm starving."

Everyone agrees that they're ready and Memphis catches

the attention of our waitress. We place our orders and enjoy our meals, making fun of each other and talking about old times. This is what family is truly about. This feeling . . . The way we can be so free with each other and enjoy each other's company, this is living, and I can't imagine doing this with anyone besides Tripp.

"I'M STUFFED," I SAY, SITTING back and rubbing my stomach, full.

The door opens. I look over and spot Tara walking in with her boyfriend, Charles, holding a cake box with her free hand.

"Happy birthday," she shouts. "Who's ready for cake?"

Smiling, I stand up and kiss Tara on the cheek, grabbing the cake from her hand and setting it down on the table. "Thanks, Tara. You made this for me?"

She nods. "Yes, and Tripp helped. You better like it."

"I'll love it." I nod at Charles and then help him pull a table over, next to our booth.

Memphis cuts the cake and we all dive in, enjoying ourselves.

"Happy birthday, baby." Tripp slides a birthday card in front of me, but keeps her hand on it. "Before you open this, I have some news for you."

I slip my hand behind her neck and pull her to me. "The house. Did we get the fucking house?"

She nods her head and I pull her in, kissing her long and hard. "We get the key next week," she exclaims. "Everything is about to change, Alex. Are you sure you're ready for this?"

I smile and rest my forehead to hers. "With you . . . yes. I've been ready my whole life."

"Good." She smiles. "Open the card."

Everyone around the table watches me as I reach for the card and rip the envelope open. I pull the card out and read the front. It's got some kind of stick figure on it that looks like a kid's drawing. "Happy birthday, daddy."

My heart stops when I look beside me to see tears streaming down Tripp's face. "What's this?"

"Your first birthday card from your child."

"Holy fuck!" I stand up, almost knocking the table over. "You're pregnant? We're having a baby?"

Tripp nods and throws both of her hands over her mouth.

"Holy shit!" I reach for Tripp's hand and pull her up to her feet. "I love you. I love you so fucking much, baby. This is by far the best day of my life outside of the day you became my wife. You're going to be the *mother* of my child. We're doing this together."

The girls all seem to break into tears of joy and Memphis and Charles both slap me on the back, congratulating me.

"I love you too. I'm so damn happy. I wouldn't want to do this with anyone but you." She throws her head back and laughs as I bend down and kiss her belly, and then grab her face to kiss her lips. "I've known for a week. Do you know how hard it's been to wait until today to tell you?"

I shake my head and tangle my hands into the back of her hair. "I'm so ready to start a family with you. Our baby is going to have the best parents. You know that, right?"

Tripp nods her head and kisses me one last time, before the girls pull her away and start talking in their high pitched, girly voices.

"Congrats, man." Memphis throws his arms around me. "I'm so proud of you, little brother. I love you, man. The two of you are going to make great parents."

"Thanks, bro. I love you too." I grip his shoulder when we pull apart. "You're going to be a great uncle. I can only hope that my child will turn out to be anything like you."

He smiles and wraps his arm around Lyric, and that's when I take the opportunity to take my woman back.

"I love you more now than I ever have in my entire life, and I would give up everything I own to make sure that you and our child are happy and taken care of. You know that, right?"

Tripp pulls me as close as she can and buries her face into my neck. "I know you would and I would do the same. Always." She kisses my neck. "I love you."

I've loved this woman since I was eight and I will love her and our child until the day I die. That's a promise that I can keep . . .

THE END

BOOKS BY VICTORIA ASHLEY

Standalone Books

Wake Up Call

This regret

Thrust

Hard & Reckless

Strung

Sex Material

Wreck My World

Steal You Away

Walk of Shame Series

Slade

Hemy

Cale

Stone

Styx

Kash

Savage & Ink Series

Royal Savage

Beautiful Savage

Pain Series

Get Off On the Pain

Something For The Pain

Alphachat Series (Co-written with Hilary Storm)

Pay For Play

Two Can Play

Locke Brother Series (Co-written with Jenika Snow)

Damaged Locke

Savage Locke

Twisted Locke

ACKNOWLEDGMENTS

First and foremost, I'd like to say a big thank you to all my loyal readers that have given me support over the last couple years and have encouraged me to continue with my writing. Your words have all inspired me to do what I enjoy and love. Each and every one of you mean a lot to me and I wouldn't be where I am if it weren't for your support and kind words.

I'd also like to thank my friend, Author of the Fate Series and editor, Charisse Spiers. She has put a lot of time into helping me put this story together. I'm lucky to have her be a part of this journey with me. Please everyone look out for her books. She has shown me so much support through this whole process and it would be nice to be able to return the favor. Her stories are beautifully written and something that the world shouldn't miss out on.

My amazingly, wonderful PA, Amy Preston Rogers. She helped me from the very beginning of Something For The Pain and fell in love with Alex before anyone else. Her support has meant so much to me.

Also, all of my beta readers and friends that have taken the time to read my book and give me pointers throughout this process. You guys have helped encourage me more than you know. Kellie Richardson of *KinkyGirlsBookObsessions* was also amazing and kept me excited to continue with Alex's story. Thank you so much for that, Kellie! *Bestsellers and Beststellars of Romance* for hosting my cover reveal, blog tour and release day blitz. Hetty Whitmore Rasmussen has been a big part in making this happen. You all have. Thank you all so much.

Thank you to my boyfriend, friends and family for understanding my busy schedule and being there to support me through the hardest part. I know it's hard on everyone, and everyone's support means the world to me.

Last but not least, I'd like to thank all of the wonderful book bloggers that have taken the time to support my book and help spread the word. You all do so much for us authors and it is greatly appreciated. I have met so many friends on the way and you guys are never forgotten. You guys rock. Thank you!

ABOUT THE AUTHOR

Victoria Ashley grew up in Illinois and has had a passion for reading for as long as she can remember. After finding a reading app where it allowed readers to upload their own stories, she gave it a shot and writing became her passion.

She lives for a good romance book with tattooed bad boys that are just highly misunderstood. When she's not reading or writing about bad boys, you can find her watching her favorite shows.

www.victoriaashleyauthor.com

Made in the USA
Columbia, SC
17 October 2021